The Seminarian

THE ROAD BACK TO GOD

Mr. Anthony L Korey

ISBN: 1492247774
ISBN 13: 9781492247777

PART ONE:
THE SEMINARIAN'S BEGINNING
Childhood

ONE

It was the summer of 1950. Both Anthony Michael Saleem and his brother, Freddy Boy, walked through the woods behind their back yard. Jacksonville was the gateway to the east coast of Florida. The Saleem family lived in a 750-square-foot wood-framed house. The paint, which appeared to be a dingy white, was peeling to the point that it was difficult to determine the actual color. It literally had no foundation. It was supported by large, hollow stucco blocks. The back porch was both a health and physical hazard. The frame of the back porch, which was virtually rotting away, supported one healthy three-foot plank. The plank, which had been painted glossy white, was used to enter and exit the kitchen at the rear of the house.

The Saleem house began with five rooms and a single bathroom. There was only one bedroom and a single room which housed the washing machine and storage space. This was converted into a second bedroom. Fred Sr. and Ophelia slept in the first bedroom while the three children, Fred Jr., Cecelia, and Tony, slept in the makeshift bedroom. The fact that Cecelia was sleeping with two boys prompted Fred Sr., with the help of his brothers, to build an additional room in the rear of the house. This became known as "Cecelia's Bedroom". It would have been somewhat comfortable except for the fact that four months after the completion of Cecelia's bedroom Johnny Saleem came into this world.

The Saleem family was obviously very poor, but the Saleem children would not realize it until much later in life. They lived in a poorly-structured three-bedroom, one-bathroom, barely-painted wood-framed house with a rotting porch. The house sat at the corner of Herman Street and Lenox Road, at the southwest edge of the city.

It was a clear, but hot morning. The mixture of honeysuckle and moist pine tickled the senses of Tony's nose as it filled the air. Tony stopped for a moment and closed his eyes, as he took a deep breath to drink it all in.

"What the hell do you think you're doing?" Freddy Boy's abrupt shouting snapped Tony back to reality. "We're looking for the Indians' campsite, you idiot! If you want to day dream, just go back home."

Tony just looked at Freddy Boy and shrugged his shoulders. If he said anything, it would only make him madder. Freddy Boy's lips curled as he looked at his younger brother, then he turned and stomped his way forward. The two boys continued moving through the underbrush covering the back-woods.

"I think I see their camp ahead," said Freddy Boy. "Boy" distinguished him from their father, Fred Senior.

"Are you sure?" Tony asked in a trembling voice.

"You idiot!" Freddy Boy snapped. "We're only pretending! If I were really tracking Indians, I damn sure wouldn't have a jerk like you with me. Yes! I'm sure!"

"I know," Tony answered. "I was just playing, too."

"You sound like a little baby!"

"I'm not a baby! I'm seven!"

"Seven!" Freddy Boy laughed out loud. "When you grow up to be almost twelve like me, then I'll stop calling you a baby. Now, shut up! I want to play some more."

It was always the same. Freddy Boy would lure him into playing a game. Once the game got started, Fred would become a completely different person. That was when he would start to get mean.

"Okay! Get ready, men!" Fred said as if he were speaking to an entire regiment of troops. "Prepare to attack!"

Tony just stood there, holding his pretend rifle, which happened to be a three-foot long piece of tree limb. Freddy Boy looked down at Tony, the sneer spreading across his face.

"You are nothing but a worthless piece of crap!" Freddy Boy yelled, grabbing Tony by the collar; he jerked him forward and tore off the button of his shirt. "You don't even know how to hold a rifle in the attack position." He then flung Tony down the four-foot embankment in front of them.

Tony jerked his arms in front of his face to break the fall. His right forearm caught the protruding end of a jagged rock. Tony screamed as he grabbed his bleeding arm.

"See! I told you that you were nothing but a cry baby!" Freddy Boy laughed.

"What's wrong?" Cecelia screamed as she came running.

Freddy Boy's face turned pale white. He was terrified of his younger sister.

"He threw me down here!" Tony shouted.

"He's nothing but a rotten liar! He fell. I didn't throw him. I never touched him."

"I think my arm is broken!" Tony cried out as he climbed up the bank, holding his forearm.

"You're bleeding," Cecelia moaned, carefully studying his cut arm. "Wiggle your fingers."

Tony did.

"I don't think it's broken, and I feel sure that you're going to be okay."

Cecelia spoke with such professionalism and confidence, it immediately calmed Tony's fears.

"Come on, we'll show it to Emma," Cecelia said, leading Tony back to the house. "She'll take care of it."

"Emma" was the Lebanese word for "mother." Ophelia Saleem was their matri-arch. She was not only their mother, she was also their doctor, nurse, housekeeper, cook, and everything else that goes with being the mother of four children. Her husband, Fred, was a heavy-equipment operator for the City of Jacksonville Public Works Department. They had moved to Jacksonville from Pittsburgh a little over five years ago. It was just after the war had ended.

It was always said that they had moved to the warmer Florida climate because of Ophelia's health. The truth, however, was because of Fred's health, and it had nothing to do with the climate. Fred was either already an alcoholic, or was rapidly on the path to alcoholism. During the war, he was deferred from military duty because of the necessity of his civilian job—that of driving trucks. He would transport bombs from the munitions factories in Pittsburgh, Pennsylvania, to the shipping ports of New York and New Jersey. Many times he would transport the explosives to the Naval Yards of Richmond, Virginia. The long, lonely hours, coupled with the stress of the cargo, turned him to alcohol for both relief and sanity.

Once the war ended, Ophelia gave him an ultimatum. He would either stop drinking or find another family. It had been three years since his last drink. He traded his bomb-moving trucks in for machinery that moved construction materials, as well as the very earth itself. Fred happily accepted his new job and new responsibilities. Ophelia gratefully accepted her newly-changed husband. Fred Joseph Saleem was a man of commitment and principle. His word truly was his bond. Everything he did, after that, was aimed at fulfilling that singular promise.

Both Fred and Ophelia loved their children very much. Their family meant everything. Their youngest, Johnny, was barely a year old and consumed most of their time. Their oldest, Freddy Boy, was definitely a "mama's boy." He seemed to have her wrapped around his little finger, just like the cord had been wrapped around his neck when he was born. The deprivation of oxygen to his brain only sparked in her the desire to fill him with the breath of her love and care. Cecelia, on the other hand, was a "daddy's girl." The natural instinct of a father's love for his daughter was fulfilled by everything that Cecelia said and did. In Fred's eyes, she absolutely was his princess; she could do no wrong. Tony was the mystery child. Although his parents loved him, it always seemed, to him, that he constantly had to win over their approval.

"Emma! Emma!" Cecelia cried out as she approached the backdoor of their white-frame house.

"What is it?" Ophelia asked, pushing open the screen door.

"Tony's got a cut on his arm."

"I swear he did it himself, Emma! He tripped and fell. I didn't push him like he says." Freddy Boy's eyes narrowed as he glanced towards Tony.

"Let me look." Ophelia wiped her hands on her apron and walked towards them.

"It's just a small cut," she calmly declared. "I'll put some iodine on it, and we'll bandage it. I'm sure you'll be okay." She then smiled and gently kissed Tony on the forehead.

"Thank you, Emma," Tony said softly. "He did push me. You can ask Cecelia."

After she tended to Tony's wound, Ophelia sent Fred to his room for the rest of the day. "Even if you only bumped him, accidently, you cannot lie to me about your brother being hurt. Do you understand?"

"Yes." Freddy Boy lowered his eyes and turned to go to his room.

"If this happens, again," Ophelia said, sharply, "then I'll tell your father the moment he gets home. For now, you'll stay in your room for the rest of the day."

It was on a damp August day of that same year that seven-year-old Anthony Michael Saleem would face the first crossroad in his life. Once more, the smell of honeysuckle filled the morning air. The weeping willow tree spread out its branches and nearly covered the entire front yard. Tony sat quietly on the front porch swing, petting Spotty, his black and white cat.

"Come on!" Freddy Boy called to Tony as he pushed through the front screen door, letting it slam shut. "Let's go play in the woods."

"I really don't want to." Tony continued to stroke his cat. "You play too rough."

"Aw, don't be a sissy all of your life. Okay, I promise to go easy on you."

"I still don't want to. I'd rather stay here and just pet Spotty." Tony smiled as he stroked his cat.

"You'd rather be here, doing nothing with that stupid cat, instead of playing with your brother?" Freddy Boy's voice was both taunting and threatening.

"I guess so," Tony said.

"Emma! Emma!" Fred yelled to his mother. "Emma! Tony won't play with me! I think he hates me!"

"Tony!" Ophelia shouted from inside the house. "Be nice to your brother. Go play with him!"

"Well, little brother." Fred's mouth twisted into a sinister smile; "I guess you have to dump that stupid cat and play with me."

"I might have to play with you," Tony said, defiantly, "but Spotty is coming, too."

"Suit, yourself." Fred ran towards the back of the house and towards the woods. Tony slowly followed.

Tony recognized, despite his own young age, that Freddy Boy was slower than most twelve-year-old kids. He didn't understand things as quickly as he should. He also knew that he should treat him a lot nicer, but Freddy Boy did not like to be treated nice himself. He'd rather people be afraid of him. Fear and respect—those were the goals. In Tony's seven-year-old mind, he knew that he should love his older brother, but he wasn't sure he could, much less did. He knew that he was afraid of him—exactly as Freddy Boy would have preferred.

"Come on, slow poke!" Fred yelled, looking back. "If you got rid of that stupid cat, you could keep up!"

Tony ignored Freddy Boy and continued walking and petting Spotty as he cradled him in his arms. Suddenly Freddy Boy turned and rushed them. His actions were so abrupt, Tony's eyes widened and his body became rigid. Freddy Boy grabbed Spotty and jerked him from Tony's arms.

"This'll help you keep up!" Freddy Boy snarled as he flung the cat towards the back yard. "Now, get moving, you little asshole!" he screamed as he shoved the back of Tony's shoulder.

Although somewhat smaller than his brother, Tony was a lot faster, and smarter. Tony turned and rushed to retrieve his cat.

"I'm going to tell Emma what you did!" Tony shouted at Freddy Boy.

The sun now shone brightly on the two boys. They stood between the edge of their backyard and the wood line. Its rays flickered across the drops of dew that still clung to the pine trees. The light bounced across a metallic object less than a yard in front of them.

Freddy Boy caught the glint, and his lips curled. He quickly retrieved the metal object with his right hand. It was a rusted windshield wiper, with sharp, jagged edges. Freddy Boy's eyes widened, a cynical smile played across his lips and his nostrils flared.

"What's that?" Tony asked in a trembling voice.

"It's nothing," Fred said, as he quietly walked towards Tony and Spotty. "But it sure looks interesting."

If Tony was smarter and faster, Fred was sneaky and manipulative. His movements were slow and calculating, and he kept his shoulder slightly turned away as he advanced, keeping the article just out of Tony's sight. Tony cautiously moved towards Freddy Boy.

Freddy Boy made his move.

"I'm gonna teach your crazy cat a lesson!" Fred jerked the cat from Tony's hands once more.

"Give him back to me!"

"Oh, you'll get him back alright!" Freddy Boy spat venomous words. "I'll give him back to you one piece at a time. Which do you want first?" he asked as he raised the windshield wiper.

Tony's heart pounded in his ears and the blood rushed to his head. His right hand fumbled frantically as he searched for something to stop his brother. His fingers touched a clump of hardened clay mixed with North Florida soil. He quickly grabbed it and flung it at Freddy Boy. It stuck him on the left forearm, barely missing Spotty's torso. Freddy turned the cat loose to gape at his forearm.

Spotty buried his hind feet into the shirt and flesh just above Freddy Boy's belt-line. Across the boy's face and nose, the cat let loose his claws. Freddy Boy screamed.

"Get him off! Get him off!" The screams didn't end

Tony quickly grabbed his cat and pulled him away. Tony smiled as Freddy Boy wiped the blood and tears from his lacerated face.

"I be…I bet…I bet you think this is funny!" Fred said as he choked back the sobs. "I'll show you what's funny, you piece of shit!"

"Freddy, what's wrong? Are you alright?" Emma's voice could be heard throughout the neighborhood as she rushed from the house.

"Now it's my turn!" Freddy Boy's voice was filled with scorn and contempt as he lashed himself across his stomach with the jagged end of the windshield wiper. It cut through his shirt and broke the skin, causing blood to ooze out. He then threw the windshield wiper at Tony's feet.

"You're crazy! You're completely nuts!" Tony looked at his brother with complete disbelief.

That whipped Freddy Boy into frenzy.

Fred's nostrils flared, his eyes burned with rage, he clenched his fists and snarled like a wild animal. "I'll kill you! You bastard, I will kill you and your damn cat!"

"My God!" Ophelia stopped dead in her tracks as she looked at Freddy Boy. His face was now covered in tears, blood, and sweat. The blood was still oozing from the cut to his stomach. "Freddy, my baby! What happened to you?"

"He did it!" His finger pointed directly at Tony. "He and that cat did this to me, Emma."

Ophelia turned and looked directly at Tony, who held his cat.

"How could you do this to my son?" she screamed.

"He's lying, Emma." Tony's voice was wavering.

"Shut up!" Ophelia snapped. "You little bastard!"

Tony's jaw dropped and his arms weakened. He let Spotty fall from his arms. This was the first time she'd cursed at him. He had never seen her upset like this.

"I'm sorry, Emma," Tony said in a soft and timid voice.

"He's not really sorry," Freddy Boy said, playing the victim. "You need to punish him, Emma. He and his cat need to be punished."

"I need to take care of you," Ophelia said. She lifted Freddy's shirt to diagnose his wound. "I need to put some mercurochrome and peroxide on that cut. It might be infected. I also need to bandage it." She then took Freddy by the hand and gently led him back to the house.

Once Freddy Boy was patched up, her attention immediately turned to Tony.

"Did you hit him with that windshield wiper?"

"No, Emma! I did not. He did it to himself." Tony's eyes welled up with tears. He was about to be sent to his room for the rest of the day.

"Why are you lying? Why can't you just tell me the truth?" She glared at Tony. "Do you think you can do anything you want and just lie your way out of it?"

"No, Emma. I'm not lying! Please believe me!" Tony pleaded with his mother. "Freddy Boy is the one that's lying. He just wants to get me in trouble."

Tony caught a glimpse of Freddy Boy walking over. He had the biggest and most sadistic looking smile on his face. Ophelia's back was turned away as he gave Tony the finger. He then mouthed the words "cry baby" as he pretended to be wiping his eyes.

"Get me a switch from the willow tree," she told Freddy.

"Gladly, Emma. Can I watch?"

"Emma," Tony's voice quivered. "Aren't you going to send me to my room?"

She didn't answer him. Fred returned with the biggest switch he could find.

"Take off all of your clothes," she told Tony.

"What?"

"You will be punished for what you did! Now take off all of your clothes, or I will do it!"

Tony, reluctantly, stripped to his shorts and tee shirt.

"I said all of your clothes!!!" she screamed directly into Tony's face.

Tony turned pale white, and tears began to roll down his cheeks.

Freddy Boy was now licking his lips and drooling as he stood behind Emma.

It was the most brutal and vicious beating that Tony had ever received, or would ever receive. It went well beyond punishment, beyond abuse. It would have fit more in the classification of a sadistic attempted murder. At one point, when the switch broke against Tony's bloody backside, she continued the beating with the rusted windshield wiper which Freddy Boy handed her. She continued beating him until her seven-year-old son succumbed to unconsciousness.

TWO

Dr. Leo G. Temples was the Saleem family's physician, and he had been ever since they first moved to Jacksonville. He had a special relationship with them, as they were his very first patients. He had been a doctor in the Army Medical Corps, but once the war ended, he decided to set up a private practice on Lee Street in Jacksonville, Florida. While he was still in the process of moving into his office, Fred Sr. came to him and told him that his wife was pregnant. He saw the sign out front, and he was hoping that he could help him. Dr. Temples advised him that his office was not ready, but he would be glad to make a house call. That was all it took. After that they became not only his permanent patients but also his permanent friends.

Dr. Temples was everyone's version of what a doctor should look like. He was six feet tall and a trim 180 pounds. He'd been a running back for the University of Florida, where he went on to receive his medical degree. He did his residency at St. Vincent's Hospital in Jacksonville. In fact the only time he had been out of the state was when he was drafted into the military. Except for the distinguishing gray around his temples, he didn't look a day over thirty five. In reality, he was pushing forty six. Dr. Leo G. Temples was decent man and an extremely honest and ethical physician— but right now, the Saleem family needed his help.

"At least he's stable, for now." Dr. Temples' words were not spoken with much confidence.

"Do you think he's going to make it?" Fred Sr. asked.

"I'm not sure. He's stable. Right now prayer is his best medicine."

"Father Peter Paul is on his way. I called the church and told him what happened." Fred Sr.'s voice cracked and he began to sob. "I thought…" Tears streamed down his face. "I thought he might need to be given the last rites." He put his face in his hands as the tears flowed.

Dr. Temples gently put his arm around Fred's shoulders.

"I can't believe that she would do this to her own son." Fred began to shake. "What kind of person would do this to their own baby?"

Because of their years-long relationship, Leo Temples understood their physical health better than anyone on earth. When the vein in Fred Sr.'s forehead begin to protrude, the doctor knew that he was overwhelmed with stress. When he saw the muscles in his neck begin to protrude, he knew that he was at risk of a stroke.

"Let's go to the living room, and talk."

Fred only nodded.

"Where are the rest of the children?" Dr. Temples asked.

"I had my brother Joe come and get them. I did not want them to see all of this."

"That was good thinking. Where is Ophelia?"

"She's in the bedroom, praying." Fred answered. "She thinks God's going to forgive her for this."

Fred Sr. looked at Leo with pleading eyes. His face was covered with a mixture of sweat and tears, and his hands were shaking. He'd come home from work hot and tired and sweaty. He then asked where the kids were. When Ophelia did not answer, he knew that something was wrong.

"What if he dies?" Fred asked.

"We are going to do our best to make sure that does not happen," Dr. Temples answered, reassuringly.

"What am I supposed to do if he dies?" Fred insisted.

Dr. Temples' face took on a puzzled look. He then realized exactly what Fred Sr. was asking.

"The police will want to know the cause of death. I would lose my license if I lie to them." Leo Temples took Fred's calloused hand. "The first thing we have to do, my dear friend, is do everything we can to keep him alive."

Fred nodded in agreement.

"Once we do that," Dr. Temples continued, "it then becomes your responsibility to find out why this happened and to keep it from ever happening again."

Their conversation was interrupted by a loud pounding at the door. Fred immediately walked over and opened it for Father Peter J. Paul. Father Peter Paul was a huge mass of a man. He stood more than 6'6" tall. Although he did not have an ounce of fat on him, he weighed in at 297 pounds. Even with the streaming white hair, he did not look like a sixty five year-old man.

"How is Tony?" Father Paul's rough voice made it seem as if he were mad all the time.

"According to the doctor, he's stable."

"I've never trusted doctors!"

"Father," Fred said nervously. "I'd like you to meet Leo Temples. I mean, Doctor Leo Temples. He's Tony's doctor."

"You make house calls?" Father Paul stuck out a huge right hand.

"Yes," answered Dr. Temples, grasping the priest's enormous hand with both of his. "It is an absolute pleasure to meet you, Father."

"I'm sorry about the remark," Father Paul laughed. "You seem like a trustworthy person, especially if you make house calls."

"Thank you."

"May I see Tony?" The priest asked. "If I have to give him the last rites, I do not want to delay."

"I understand," Dr. Temples answered. "I'll take you to him."

"Where's the rest of your family?" Father Paul asked Fred Sr. as they walked to Tony's bedroom.

"The kids are at Joe's," Fred answered. "Ophelia's in our bedroom."

Father Paul only nodded. Dr. Temples pushed open the door to Tony's room. The priest froze. He slowly raised his hand to his mouth. The seven-year-old child resembled a miniaturized mummy. As he lay on his stomach, all that was revealed were bandages covering every inch of his entire backside. From his shoulders to the bottom of his feet, he was wrapped in gauze and tape.

"My, God!" Father Paul uttered. "How could she do this!?" He walked slowly to Tony's bedside. He then set his black bag on the edge of the bed. He opened the bag and pulled the purple stole, which he kissed and placed around his neck. He then pulled out the white linen cloth and the small bottle of olive oil. The olive oil had been blessed by the bishop of the diocese on Holy Thursday. It was to be used exclusively for the sacrament of *extreme unction,* "the blessing of the extremely ill." It was also known as the *last rites.*

After Father Peter Paul completed the administering of the sacrament, he returned the olive oil and stole to his bag and shut it. He then grabbed the bag by its handles and looked at Dr. Temples.

"I guess we both have these black bags for the same reason," Father Paul noted sadly.

"I guess so." Dr. Temples nodded.

Father Paul walked with Fred and Dr. Temples to the kitchen table.

"I can try to make us some coffee," Fred said in an unsure tone.

"I'll do it." Ophelia slowly stepped into the room.

Both Father Peter Paul and Dr. Temples stood up as she entered the room, though the gesture did not carry respect this night. She immediately grabbed Father Paul's hand and kissed it as she went to one knee. Father Paul raised her to a standing position.

"Coffee would be wonderful," said the massive priest.

Her face was still wet with tears and her eyes were bright red with anguish. She looked deep into the priest's eyes. What few tears were left began to flow once more. He simply nodded. He then gently pulled and embraced her with his massive arms. His gentleness gave her permission to let go. Her entire body shook as she cried out.

"My God! My God! What have I done?" The reality of her actions began to overwhelm her. Her legs became weak and she began to crumble.

Father Paul gently lifted her and sat her in a chair.

"You have to compose yourself." His voice was soft and calming. "Right now, you need rest. I'm sure the good doctor here can give you something.

Dr. Temples started to rise, but Ophelia placed her hand on his knee to stop him.

"No! No!" She vigorously shook her head. "I need to make coffee, and then I need to be with Tony." She rose from the chair and immediately went to the stove. "I'll have plenty of time for rest after I die."

Once she finished making and serving the coffee, she went straight to Tony's room and stood at the entrance. She turned her head and looked back at her husband. Her eyes were pleading for his permission. He simply nodded. She smiled and breathed a sigh of relief. Entering the room, she shut the door.

"You did the right thing." Father Paul gently touched Fred's right shoulder.

"I hope so," Fred replied. "Thank you for keeping her calm. You have a gift for dealing with people. You're what every priest should be like."

"No," laughed Father Peter Paul. "I'm what every priest becomes when they get too damned old to do anything else."

The three men laughed, but quickly caught themselves before they disturbed Tony.

"Were you a military chaplain?" Dr. Temples asked

The priest smiled, as he shook his head. "No, I was never in the military. Why do you ask?"

"You seem very familiar."

"Well, you don't seem familiar to me," Father Paul laughed.

"I guess it's your name, and I've seen your picture before. I just can't quite place it."

"Father Peter Paul was here when I first came to Florida," Fred Sr. said. "He came from Ettal, a Dominican Monastery in Germany. Go ahead, Father. Tell him the story of how you came to the States. Unless you're too shy?"

There was one basic fact about Father Peter Paul: he could never be accused of being shy. If anything, he was brashly outspoken. Father Peter Paul cherished three special things. The first was his love of God. The second was his love of people. And the third was his love to tell a story.

Father Paul took a sip of his coffee, leaned forward, and placed his elbows on the kitchen table. He loved putting drama into each and every tale. He loved the fact that he could capture an audience, even an audience of one. He closely looked at Leo Temples' eyes. Before he could say a word, however, Dr. Temples suddenly sat straight up and clapped his hands.

"Now I know!" Dr. Temples said, a little too loud. "I'm sorry," he said, as he quickly calmed himself, looking towards Tony's room. "You're Father Peter J. Paul! You're the one who helped Dietrich Bonhoeffer smuggle all of those Jewish families out of Germany. You're a war hero and a saint."

Father Paul was visibly blushing. His face turned bright red, and beads of sweat were forming on his brow.

"You never told me about this," Fred Sr. said, a puzzled look on his face.

"I guess it slipped my mind," Father Paul Said. "But you are mistaken, my friend. It was Bonhoeffer who was the war hero. He was the true saint. He was a martyr. I'll never forget the day that he and I were betrayed by that bastard, Johannes Kaffee. It's hard to believe, a man like that was actually a Brother in the Benedictine Order. He was nothing but a cowardly piece of dog crap, a Nazi collaborator!"

Father Peter J. Paul then paused and noted with satisfaction: he actually had both Dr. Temples and Fred Sr. sitting on the edges of their seats. He was truly a master storyteller.

"I was one of twenty-two Augustinian Cannons, who had been assigned to the Benedictine Monastery known as Ettal," he began. "Dietrich, on the other hand, was a protestant. He was the leader of the anti-Nazi group known as the Confessing

Church. They were a radical group who were very outspoken against Adolph Hitler and his tactics of genocide.

"We, however, had been told by our Catholic leaders to be very low key—to stay away from all political controversy. Controversy, hell!" The priest raised his voice, then immediately toned it down. "They were killing Jews by the millions. That's not political controversy. That's *mass murder!*" Father Paul took another sip of his coffee and emptied his cup. Fred Sr. immediately refilled it for him.

"Please, continue," he said, eager to hear more.

Father Paul nodded. Continuing in a deceptively quiet voice, he began by first painting an exquisite word picture to describe the beauty of Ettal, the stage upon which his drama would begin.

THREE

Located eight miles southeast of Munich, Germany, Ettal was a Benedictine monastery and the most beautiful of all structures in and around Bavaria. Known as "Bayern", Bavaria was the largest and most beautiful state in Germany, well-endowed with natural riches: snowy Alpine peaks, rushing streams and velvety forests. It also had a wealth of historic buildings, some dating back to the fourteenth century. The Abbey of Ettal Monastery had looked out over the countryside since the early 1300's. It had burned down in 1744, but was rebuilt in a beautiful baroque style, accented by the green-domed central cathedral and abbey.

But on this crucial day in history, the absolute silence which engulfed this magnificent edifice was broken by the roaring sound of a dozen planes overhead. Father Peter Paul's face grimaced as he looked at the planes bearing down from Munich.

"What's wrong?" asked Dietrich Bonhoeffer, the visiting protestant pastor.

"I truly don't know," answered the Augustinian priest. "I feel as if something very evil occupies those planes."

Father Peter Paul was a man of uncanny instincts. He was gifted with an ability to sense evil lurking in the world around him, an ability that bordered on the supernatural. And in this case, Father Paul's senses revealed the horrible truth: this squadron flew as security for a small passenger plane cradled in the center of their formation.

"I believe you are correct in your assumption," answered Bonhoeffer. "The plane in the middle is the personal aircraft of Germany's leader."

Father Paul's mouth tightened, his lips thinning as he watched the Messerschmitt pass overhead. "I pray that you and the Abwehr will someday be able to free Germany of this anti-Christ."

Bonhoeffer became pale as a ghost as he turned. "You must never say that out loud, again, my dear compatriot. If anyone ever heard those words, it could mean the death of both of us, and the death of the entire Abwehr."

"The Ab… what?" asked Fred, interrupting Father Paul's story.

"That's right," Father Paul answered. "You never were in the military; were you, my dear friend?" he said, as he patted Fred on the shoulder.

Fred shook his head and smiled.

"The Abwehr was the intelligence section of German military," said Father Paul, as he looked directly at Fred. "In fact, I think that they were the only ones with any intelligence," laughed Father Peter Paul.

Fred looked confused.

"They were actually involved with Dietrich in the planning of Hitler's assassination. In my mind that makes them extremely intelligent," Father Paul explained.

Fred nodded indicating his understanding.

"You see," Peter Paul continued. "Bonhoeffer helped the Abwehr, and the Abwehr helped Bonhoeffer."

"How?" asked Dr. Temples.

"Bonhoeffer was the one who developed the entire plan on how to execute Adolph Hitler!" he answered.

"I never knew that," Dr. Temples said. "How did the Abwehr help Dietrich Bonhoeffer?"

"Great question," smiled Father Paul. "They helped him in the rescue of thousands of Jewish families. The Abwehr provided the funds and Bonhoeffer set up the underground transportation of the Jewish families to Switzerland and the United States."

Father Peter Paul took another sip of coffee, as he relished in the knowledge that he was mesmerizing both Dr. Temples and Fred.

"Let me continue," Father Paul said.

"Of course," Fred said as he moved a little closer to this massive priest, not wanting to miss a single word that came out of his mouth.

"I wish all of my parishioners were this attentive, especially on Sunday morning," laughed Father Paul.

"In any case, I told Dietrich that I did not mean to upset him." Father Paul's words were filled with sincerity. "But we are in the middle of a field. The closest human to us is two hundred meters away, and he has taken the vow of silence."

Bonhoeffer burst into laughter as he embraced Father Paul. "You truly are dear to me. I love you so much that I continuously pray that you will someday join the Confessing Church."

"And I truly do admire you and the Confessing Church, Dietrich." Father Paul smiled. "You and your colleagues are a brave group of pastors. I only wish that we would be allowed to be as outspoken."

"Don't be so impatient, my dear father," sighed Bonhoeffer. "Your cardinal is very conservative and likes to use diplomacy."

"There's a difference between diplomacy and appeasement, however," Father Paul retorted. "You can't appease that," he said, pointing to the aircraft flying above. "You have to kill it."

Dietrich Bonhoeffer grimaced, quickly looking around to see if anyone heard. He then grasped Father Paul's arm and whispered ever so quietly.

"Soon, my precious friend. It will be soon."

Father Peter Paul smiled.

"We can continue this conversation as we walk to our quarters," said Bonhoeffer.

"I'm sure you are anxious to get back to your writings," Father Paul said as he began walking with Bonhoeffer. "How is the book coming along?"

"It is tedious and slow," answered Bonhoeffer. "But it is a true justification."

Dietrich Bonhoeffer was writing a book on ethics. In actuality, he was justifying the killing of Adolph Hitler. He would bring his reader to the conclusion that the only possible alternative for the defense of every Jewish person and every decent person on the face of this earth was the justifiable killing of pure evil. That evil was Adolph Hitler.

"I am sure that it is," answered Father Paul. "The confronting of absolute evil cannot be limited to the ethical guidelines of innocence."

The walk to the quarters of the Augustinian Cannons of Ettal was very refreshing. As both Bonhoeffer and Father Paul entered the green-domed abbey, they quietly took the stairs to the second floor and turned down the hallway to their rooms. They did not notice that the room next to Father Peter Paul's was being cleaned by Brother Johannes Kaffee.

Benedictine brothers were those who had not attained the level of monk or priest, and they probably never would. They were those individuals who desired the monastic life but did not have the educational ability to become ordained as a priest. Brother Johannes Kaffee was such a person. He felt inferior to the monks and the priests, and he knew they felt superior to him. He was a man filled with anger and bitterness, and he lurked silently around corners to watch and weigh the life he so heavily coveted.

"Well, here we are," said Father Paul. "Do you want to step in for a moment?"

"I sincerely appreciate the offer," answered Bonhoeffer; "but I must get back to my writing. However, I must ask you to make another delivery."

"Certainly!"

Dietrich Bonhoeffer unbuttoned his shirt and removed a large manila envelope. He then looked to either end of the hallway to see if anyone else was watching or listening. He had no way of knowing that Brother Johannes stood underneath the open transom. Feeling relatively safe, Bonhoeffer handed the envelope to Father Paul.

"Please do not be shocked by what it contains," warned Bonhoeffer. "These are desperate times for our Jewish friends. Radical measures are needed."

Brother Johannes Kaffee's heart skipped a beat. *Jewish friends. Radical measures.*

"My God! There must be several hundred thousand marks here! Where did you get such money?"

"Friends in the Abwehr collected most of it," Bonhoeffer said. "I am so sorry I got you involved in this, Father," he continued "but you were the only one that I could trust."

"Never apologize for that!" Father Paul said with a firm voice. "You truly are a courageous man of God, Dietrich Bonhoeffer. You not only risk your freedom, but also your very life in helping people whom you do not even know. I am honored to be part of this."

The seasoned Catholic priest's eyes began to well up. It was the first time in their longtime friendship that Bonhoeffer had ever seen him cry.

"Shall I handle this same as always, or does it need some special treatment?" Father Paul asked.

"No special treatment," Bonhoeffer answered. "Just give it to our banker friend in Munich. He will know what to do."

"Karl Gerhard?"

Bonhoeffer looked shocked as he quickly scanned the halls again.

"Do not be so paranoid, my friend. This place is a refuge from evil," laughed the priest.

"I suppose you are right," Bonhoeffer gave a sigh of relief.

Brother Johannes laughed to himself, as he furiously wrote every word on a tablet.

"Tell Karl," Bonhoeffer said, still whispering, "that he is to begin the travel arrangements for the large group that he and I discussed earlier."

It would be this statement, just a short time in the future, that would not only lead to deadly consequences for Dietrich Bonhoeffer but also have a profound impact upon the not-yet-born Anthony Michael Saleem.

Brother Johannes Kaffee's lips curved as he continued to write. "It is, as if God, Himself, were responsible for this!"

FOUR

"Father, please come quickly." Ophelia's voice was filled with panic.

Father Paul turned toward the bedroom door from his place at the table.

"What is it?"

"It's Tony." Her voice began to tremble.

He immediately rose from the table and went straight into Tony's room. Both Fred and Dr. Temples followed him.

"He started asking for you," Ophelia said.

"Father Peter Paul," Tony said as he tried to raise his head.

"I'm here. I'm here beside you"

"What happened to me?"

"You are very sick," Father Paul said softly.

"Am I going to die?"

"Only God knows that, my son."

"Will you stay here with me?"

"Of course," his voice began to crack. "I'll stay as long as necessary."

Father Peter Paul then looked towards Fred and Dr. Temples.

"I'll stay here until he falls asleep."

Fred nodded. He and Dr. Temples turned to leave the room, Fred taking Ophelia's arm.

"Emma..."Tony's voice was almost inaudible.

"Tony, Tony, I'm here."

"Please stay with me. I don't want to die without you here."

"You are not going to die," Ophelia said with a raised voice.

Fred gently touched her shoulder; he and Dr. Temples walked out.

"I will not let him die," Ophelia said to the priest.

"All we can do is pray," Father Paul answered.

Ophelia then dropped to her knees, pulling out her rosary beads. Every so often her prayers were interrupted by her own sobs. She stayed on her knees praying and begging God to save her son until the early morning hours.

As the morning light shown through the windows in Tony's room Ophelia covered her eyes. Father Peter Paul had already gone, promising to return later that day. Dr. Temples also left, but he would come back to check on Tony.

"Emma." Tony was able to lift his head a few inches as he whispered. "My God." His eyes widened. "Your hair is white!"

She touched the top of her head, pulled down some of hair, and looked at it. She then smiled.

"Don't be afraid," she said. "This is a sign from God."

Tony looked puzzled. He tried to turn on his side, but he let out a sharp scream of pain. Fred burst into the room and grabbed Ophelia's arm. He lifted his hand, as if to strike her.

"Daddy, don't!" Tony yelled.

"You're right," Fred said as he released his wife.

"What's happening?" Tony's voice was on the edge of tears.

"We'll explain everything when you get better," Fred lied. He knew in his heart that this was something that he could not explain. Even he did not understand it. He hoped and prayed that God would remove the events of that day from Tony's mind forever.

"You need your rest now," Fred said to his son. "We'll be back in a little while with your breakfast."

Fred and Ophelia stepped into the kitchen, gently closing Tony's door behind them.

"Why did he scream?" Fred briskly asked.

"It's my hair," Ophelia said, tears running down both sides of her face.

Fred stepped back, as noticing her solid white hair for the first time. His wife was only 37. Why would a woman of 37 have snow white hair?

"This is what God did," Ophelia said. There was a glow about her. "I told God that I would dedicate Tony to Him, for the rest of his life, if He would let him live." Ophelia wiped tears from her eyes. "I then knew that God wanted a sacrifice for my sin. I was going to give God that sacrifice. I always loved my black hair."

"What were you going to do?" Fred spoke with compassion and care.

"I was going to cut it off; but I knew that it would grow back. My only sacrifice would be a couple of months of shame. I had to do more."

Fred brushed the right side of her hair with his hand. He was a gentle man, and it broke his heart to see his wife in so much agony. He yearned to comfort her. He gently touched her cheek and wiped a tear with his thumb.

"Why would God want to hurt you?" Fred asked. "I still love you. Tony still loves you. I know that a loving God absolutely still loves you."

The floodgates opened. Tears freely flowed down her cheeks. She choked back her sobs and buried her face into his chest, as she clung to him. She tried to muffle her cries of agony. She did not want to disturb Tony.

"But this is a sign," she said with a broken voice. "God did not want me to sacrifice anything. He showed His love by keeping me from cutting it off. He also wanted to remind me of this sin that I have committed. God did not want me to ever forget it. Oh, Farreed! Farreed!" Farreed was Fred's name in Arabic. "What have I done? Will I ever be forgiven? Will I ever know if God has forgiven me?"

Fred wrapped her in his arms, but sadly, he did not say a word.

FIVE

It took twenty-one days for Tony's wounds to heal. Tony spent the remainder of the summer at Our Lady of the Angels Catholic Church, working with Father Peter Paul. The priest had grown very fond of Tony. Tony's feelings were mutual.

Father Paul would take Tony to the beach at least twice a week. He would often take him to an afternoon movie. The rest of the time Tony spent studying religion and Latin under the tutelage of Father Marcus De Chico, the associate pastor of Our Lady of the Angels Catholic Church.

Father De Chico looked diminutive when he stood beside his pastor, Father Peter Paul. Father De Chico was a likeable priest, but he lacked the charisma of the out-spoken Peter Paul. He was, however, a gifted teacher. Tony excelled in his classes at school as a direct result of Father De Chico's tutoring.

The routine of Tony being dropped off by his father at 6:00 a.m. every morning at Our Lady of the Angels continued for the next seven years. Either Father De Chico or Father Peter Paul would then take Tony at 8:00 a.m. to Immaculate Conception Catholic School on weekdays. They would also pick him up at 3:00 p.m. sharp and return to the church, where Tony would study and play.

Fred did everything he could to protect his son. When Freddy Boy dropped out of school and joined the Army at the age of seventeen, only then did Fred Senior begin to relax his routine. He arranged for Tony to go to the church on weekends, rather than every day.

On June 25, 1955, three days after Tony's twelfth birthday, he was in the church choir loft helping Father Peter Paul repair the baseboards. Father Paul was in the sanctuary repairing the baseboard which was directly beneath the choir loft. It was just turning dark when Tony had a strange and uneasy feeling. Looking out over the rest of the church, he saw two men walking into the sanctuary. He went to yell out, but a strange sense of fear came over him. One was tall and lanky with greasy blond hair and appeared to be in his twenties. The other one appeared to be the same age but walked with a slight limp. He was much shorter than the first and his skin was darker. The shorter one with dark skin appeared to be holding something in his right hand.

As they passed directly beneath him, Tony froze. He could clearly see what the short one held. He had a gun.

"May I help you?" It was the voice of Father Peter Paul.

Both men turned towards the right side of the sanctuary and looked in Father Paul's direction, directly beneath the choir loft. Tony quickly and silently ducked behind the solid railing, praying that he was not noticed.

Tony raised his head just enough over the edge of the railing and he saw the short one raise his gun.

"Get over here!" He end his sentence with a curse.

"How dare you use such language in the house of God!" said Father Peter Paul, coming into Tony's view.

"Drop that damn hammer!" snapped the taller blond man as he pulled a chrome plated gun from beneath his shirt. "Drop it or I'll blow your fucking head off!"

"I'm a priest. I have no intention of causing you any harm," Father Peter Paul said as he gently placed the hammer on the pew. He then raised his hands and slowly moved between the pews towards the two men. "What is it you want?"

"Money!" sneered the shorter one. "We want your money, you piece of dog waste! What the hell do you think we want?"

"I don't have any money," the priest said softly as he approached the two. "I've taken the vow of pover—"

The dull thud resounded up to the choir loft as the butt of the chrome plated gun struck the side of the priest's face. Blood shot from his mouth and splattered across the right shoulder of his cassock. Tony was horrified. He immediately clasped his hand over his mouth; and tears welled over from his eyes and down his cheeks.

"We don't care whose money it is, you old fart!" screamed the tall one. "Just give us some damn money!"

Tony watched the gentle parish priest wipe the blood from his mouth with the sleeve of his cassock. Squeezed his own right hand, Tony realized that he too was holding a hammer.

I'll only have one shot, he thought to himself. *If I could just hit one, it might give Father Paul a chance to run away, or get his hammer.*

Praying for God's direction and a miracle, he gripped the hammer even tighter.

"What money are you talking about?" said the priest.

"You are nothing but a slobbering idiot," said the shorter one, stepping up and standing on the pew in order to reach the huge priest's head. He then pushed the tip of the barrel against the priest's temple and cocked the hammer back. "How bout we start off with today's offering, you asshole! Then we'll talk about that gold cross and those gold statues up there!"

"You can't be serious?" Father Peter Paul said. "This is the house of God!"

"We ain't Catholic!" The tall one laughed. "Now, unless you want to see your God personally, and have your brains splattered across this aisle, you better start getting us that money."

Tony knew that they were directly beneath him. He would have to stand up and lean slightly forward in order to get a good angle on them. If Father Paul could only get them to take a couple of steps forward, Tony would have a much better shot, with more momentum. It was as if the elderly priest was reading his mind.

"All right," said Father Paul. "The collection money is in the office. It's this way."

As he turned, his eye caught a glimpse of Tony in the choir loft. A slight smile played across his lips. As the two thugs followed the priest, the tall one walked behind the limping short one. Tony stood up and slung the hammer with all of his might.

He prayed for guidance as he turned it loose. He thought about David and Goliath. The hammer, traveling at a speed of over 300 feet per second, would collide with the head of the taller thug with the same impact that the stone from David's sling pierced the skull of Goliath.

Father Peter Paul would later exclaim it was God Himself who directed that hammer against Satan's demons that day. It slammed firmly against the back of the tall one's skull. The force of the hammer literally split his head open. Blood splattered everywhere. The hammer's victim lunged forward with an unholy gurgling scream and slammed into the back of his limping partner. The dark skinned thug was so shocked and disoriented that he twisted himself around and dropped his gun to catch his now dead partner. Both went crashing to the marble floor. The dead man's gun slipped from his hand and slid to the priest's feet. Father Paul slowly and gently picked up the gun. He then picked up the second weapon.

"Damn it! You lump of crap!" The shorter one screamed as he struggled to free himself from the bloody body, now draped all over him. "Get the hell off of me! You piece of shit! Get the damnation off of me!"

"I don't think he can hear you," said the priest, as he stood over the two of them.

"Well, screw me," the shorter one said, as he looked up in complete disbelief at the priest who was holding both guns.

"I told you I didn't like that kind of filthy talk in the house of God," said the priest as he knelt on one knee and stuck the barrel of the thug's own gun into his mouth.

His dark skin paled. Huge beads of sweat formed on his forehead and mixed with the blood that was dripping out of his partners split skull. Tears began to well up in his eyes, which were now wide with terror.

"I… Guurg…Pl…" His speech was garbled. His voice was incoherent as he attempted to plead for his life. The priest shoved the barrel even further into the short thug's mouth.

"Father! Are you okay?" Tony shouted, as he ran down the steps of the choir loft.

Father Peter Paul looked up at Tony. His face brightened.

"My little altar boy turned rescuer." Peter Paul's voice was gentle and caring.

"Are you all right, Father?"

"I am now. Thanks to you, my son. Come over here, and stand behind me."

Tony immediately did as he was told. What happened then would forever be indelibly etched into Tony's memory. His twelve-year-old mind could never have imagined it.

As Tony stood behind this very gentle and caring massive man of God, the priest's demeanor and voice transformed into the diabolical.

"Now! Where we? You worthless waste of sperm," the priest growled. He pushed the barrel of the gun until it could go no further. He then spit the blood from his mouth directly into the eyes of the robber. The short thug tried to wipe it off, but Father Peter Paul raised his massive left hand to backhand him. The criminal was now helpless and choking on his own gun. His lips were turning blue. His eyes began to roll backwards.

"Father…" Tony could barely get the words out. "Please don't!"

The priest stopped his arm in mid strike. He then looked at Tony's tear-covered face. He then looked down at his tormenter.

"You are a very blessed man." Father Paul's words were cold and sarcastic. "You have an angel here interceding for your life. Don't worry about anything, Tony," the priest said with his familiar gentle voice. "There's no need for you to even see this. Just go into my office, and I'll be there in a minute to call the police…"

Then it seemed as if Satan reentered him.

"For these two dead bodies."

But Tony couldn't go anywhere. It was as if his feet were bolted to the floor and his body was completely frozen in place.

Father Peter Paul then pulled the gun from the man's mouth, allowing him to gasp frantically for air. He then gently turned the man's head to the right and placed the gun against his temple. He handed Tony the second gun, as if he already knew that Tony would never leave.

"What's your name?" the priest asked in a calm and deliberate voice.

"Ma…Ma…Max!" The man, still gasping for air, choked back tears.

"Well, Max. Do you want me to give you the last rights before I blow your brains out?"

"Oh, God!" Max screamed.

36

"It's a little late to be calling on Him, isn't it? Your friend here is seeing the bowels of hell, first hand. Soon you'll be joining him, Max."

The priest then leaned backwards slightly and began to put pressure on the trigger of the already cocked weapon.

"PLEASE! PLEASE! NO!" His screams were hideous and anguished at the same time. They echoed throughout the old wooden building. "DON'T KILL ME! I DON'T WANT TO DIE! PLEASE! DO ANYTHING ELSE TO ME! JUST DON'T KILL ME!"

The priest's finger seemed to freeze in place.

"Did you say, 'Do anything else'?" The priest's voice was taunting.

"YES! CUT OFF MY TONGUE! CUT OFF MY DAMNED DICK, IF YOU WANT TO! JUST, PLEASE DON'T KILL ME!"

"Now there's an idea," said the priest, as he moved the gun from Max's temple to the front of his face, just above his lips. "I'll just shoot your dick and balls off." He then pointed the barrel towards his groin.

"Just don't kill me! Just don't kill me!" Max muttered, as tears streamed from his tightly closed eyes.

The priest then pulled Max's lower lip upwards.

"If you move, you filthy piece of waste, I'll pull the trigger instantly!"

Max froze! He stopped in mid sob.

The priest continued by forcing the lip between the firing pin of the cocked hammer and the back part of the frame, where the firing pin strikes.

"Let's see how thick your mouth is. Let's see if it can save your manhood. Since your filthy mouth caused all of this, let's see if it can get you out of it."

The priest then laughed with a cackle that could have come straight from hell itself. He then slowly pulled the trigger. It snapped as it hit the cylinder. Suddenly a strange odor began to fill the church sanctuary. Max had messed all over himself.

"I guess your mouth did save you after all," said the priest. He then jerked the weapon with an upward movement, which ripped Max's lip in half. Blood squirted across his face.

Father Paul then slowly rose to his feet, and turned towards Tony as he opened the cylinder of the weapon. It was empty. Father Paul reached into the pocket of his cassock and returned the bullets to the cylinder. He winked at Tony.

"Go on into my office, Tony, and dial the operator. Tell her to give you the police."

Tony did as he was told. Moments later the police arrived. Tony still remembers the outrage of the two Irish officers, and the Italian Sergeant, when Farther Paul told them what happened.

"Those damned animals!" exclaimed one of the officers.

"Watch your tongue, O'Reily!" the sergeant admonished.

"Sorry, Sarge. I just can't believe they hit a priest and tried to rob God's own house!"

"I know," acknowledged the sergeant. "Don't worry about it, Father. You must be exhausted. You and the boy here just go on. We'll clean up and take care of this one."

"Thank you, Albert," the priest said to the Sergeant. "It has been a trying day, and I do need to get Tony home."

The sergeant then walked over and patted Tony on the shoulder.

"You did a fine job here today, son," he said, smiling at Tony. "I know it had to be difficult and scary, but you handled it well. I'd be proud to have you as one of my officers anytime."

"I'm afraid not," laughed Father Paul. "I've got other plans for him."

As Tony walked out of the church towards Father Paul's car, he could hear Max's blood-curdling screams.

"I guess the police are interrogating him," Father Paul remarked, with a slight chuckle in his voice. "Come on, Tony. I need to drive you home and tell your parents about your bravery."

It was during that drive to Tony's house that Father Peter Paul broke his bitter-sweet news: he was being reassigned to another parish.

"Where?" Tears filled Tony's eyes and his voice was cracking.

"Don't be sad. This really is good news. Let me finish."

"It can't be good news. You're leaving." Tony wiped his eyes. "I don't want to think about it. When and where?" His voice was abrupt.

"It will be next year, but we will be together again shortly after that."

Tony caught himself in mid-sob. "What are you talking about?"

He told Tony that he was being assigned to Augustinian Academy. "That's on Staten Island in New York City. I'll be the new director and prior." Augustinian Academy was a combination prep school for the wealthy and seminary for those aspiring to become Catholic priests. He explained that he was going to award Tony the Prior's Scholarship. This simply meant that Tony would begin his studies and journey on the road to becoming a Catholic priest.

SIX

The Prior's Scholarship was a once in a lifetime opportunity. Each prior of a seminary was allowed to grant one, and only one, four-year scholarship to a person of their choosing. After being awarded, the scholarship could not be taken away from the student unless he voluntarily resigned or the prior who awarded it then removed it. Once the scholarship was given it had to be completed, before another prior could award a new scholarship. This was done to protect the student from the politics of a new prior, who might favor some other student. It was also a direct violation of the Order of St. Augustine's regulations for a prior to award the scholarship to a family member.

"You're serious," Fred cried as the priest explained to Tony's parents the events at the church.

"Calm down, Fred," Ophelia admonished. "Let Father Paul finish telling us what happened."

How proud his parents looked when they were told about the police sergeant's remark and how Father Paul also thought that Tony was such a brave and courageous young man. Then the big news came.

Ophelia literally had to brace herself against Fred's arm, slowly sinking to the sofa behind her.

"A scholarship!" The words barely got out of her mouth as she began to gasp for breath.

"Ophelia!" Fred's voice was filled with concern. "Honey! Are you okay?"

Tony brought her a glass of water. "Emma, please be okay. I don't have to go, if you don't want me to."

"My God, Tony," her voice sounded desperate. "This is the most wonderful news I have ever had." She then knelt before Father Peter Paul and grasped his arm. Before he could pull away, she began kissing the ring on his hand and then pressed it against her cheek.

"You are God's messenger and angel," she said as tears flowed from her eyes. "I can now be forgiven. My son is now going to be a priest." Her hand instinctively reached for Tony's. Tears were now flowing freely down her cheeks. She then looked into his eyes.

"You will be a priest, my precious son!" Her eyes locked with his. "You will then be able to hear my confession." Her voice became raspy. "You will forgive me!" She then turned her head and looked down, as if she were ashamed. "You will never be able to tell anyone!" She gasped and then laid her head on the carpet below and broke into deep sobs.

Tony knelt beside her and made an attempt to comfort her. Fred touched Tony's shoulder and motioned for him to stand beside him. Fred gently caressed Tony's back.

"She'll be okay," Fred said. "She's a little overwhelmed with all that has happened." Fred looked down at his son and Tony looked into his eyes. He somehow knew that his father's eyes were filled with both a mixture of joy and sadness. He also knew that his mother's eyes were filled with both anxiety and fear. How did he know that? Why was he able to discern peoples' emotions? It was absolutely a talent that he did not realize he had. It was at that moment, and in that instance, that Tony realized that only God could have given him this special gift. He literally could read a person's emotions through the windows of their eyes.

And it had started with Father Peter Paul. And his confrontation with evil.

SEVEN

Born in Pennsylvania, Fred was second-generation Lebanese-American. Ophelia, however, born on the outskirts of Beirut, Lebanon, was pure Lebanese. They were brought together by means of an arranged marriage. The father of Ophelia Curi paid the father of Fred Saleem a dowry, which guaranteed US residency for his daughter. The only things that Fred and Ophelia had in common were their national origins and their Catholic faith. Now they shared a common dream of having a child who would someday become a Catholic priest. From the time Tony started public school and took his first communion, he knew the common dream united his parents. Of course, they'd wanted Freddy Boy to fulfill that dream.

Freddy Boy was a true disappointment. He never even wanted to go to church. He would steal money from his mother's purse and steal from the younger and smaller kids at school. When he asked his parents to sign for him to go into the Army, they did so without question. It was at that time that the entire Saleem family wondered if anyone in their family would ever become a priest.

Ophelia never gave up hope. She held on to a thread of belief that came from her maiden name— Ophelia Curi. The word *Curi* was the Arabic term for *Priest*. In spite of the realization that Freddy Boy would never be ordained, Ophelia still grasped at that very thin thread of her maiden name. It had come true.

She, nor anyone else in the family, including Tony himself, expected it to be him, even if she had promised him to God if his life was spared, but here it was. He was the dream child. He would totally fulfill the hopes and desires of his mother. She would finally have her priest, and she would complete her vow to God. She smiled and felt almost redeemed.

Tony loved his parents dearly and was very eager to make them proud. He also loved his Church, and he would become the first Roman Catholic Priest from the relatively new "Our Lady of the Angels" Catholic Church, in Jacksonville, Florida.

In June of 1956, Father Peter Paul was appointed as Prior and Director of Augustinian Academy. The same appointment included his elevation to Monsignor. Ordinarily a Papal Order, issued and signed by the Pope, Monsignor Paul's elevation came via a form copy. It was also done so by proxy. This order, however, was very special. It had a handwritten signature of Pope Pius XII. There was also the actual imprint of the Papal Seal, not a copy. Attached to the letter and certificate was a personally handwritten note by Pope Pius XII to his "dear friend" Peter J. Paul. The note said:

Beloved Peter,

I am honored to be able to do this. Your heroism in Ettal was above and beyond all that could be expected. I have always admired you and your faithfulness. I know that the finest of priests will come from your seminary, Augustinian Academy.

I shall always remain your personal friend,

Pius XII

When Monsignor Peter J. Paul saw the certificate, letter, and note, his hands began to shake. He then thanked God for this special blessing.

As soon as he arrived at his new station, his first official act was to send a formal letter to Anthony Michael Saleem, with a copy to his parents, offering Tony the Prior's scholarship. The scholarship would pay for Tony's tuition, room and board, as well as certain incidental expenses not to exceed $10,000 over the four-year period.

This was all done in accordance with the guidelines, established by the Order of St. Augustine in 1921 for Augustinian Academy. It was Prior Peter J. Paul, however, who got the approval of Cardinal Spellman, to add the $10,000 expense amount.

Tony, of course, immediately accepted and was scheduled to begin his training in September of 1957. It would be his first day of high school. He would have just turned fourteen. The entire Saleem family was overjoyed, with the exception of Freddy Boy.

For some unknown reason, Freddy Boy had been given a General Discharge, not an Honorable Discharge, from the Army. He was scheduled to return home one week after Tony was scheduled to leave for Staten Island. Tony, his younger brother Johnny, and his older sister Cecelia, all agreed that it was an act of God.

PART TWO: THE SEMINARIAN

LIFE IN THE SEMINARY

EIGHT

Everything is happening so fast, Tony thought, as he watched the telephone poles flick past his window.

The drive to the bus station seemed so much shorter than his initial drive home. The decision was made that he would say his goodbyes at the house and only his father would take him to the bus station. He didn't dread going back to Staten Island, he just wasn't quite ready to leave his family and his home.

He thought about Diane as they rode. Diane Mott was his neighbor. A smile lit up his face as he remembered the first time they met. It was only the summer of last year that Tony even allowed himself the luxury of really looking at a girl. She wasn't just any girl; she was, in reality, the girl next door.

"I guess those are our new neighbors," said Tony as he and his sister sat on the front porch and watched the huge semi-truck being unloaded.

"I suppose," answered Cecelia, "It's too early in the morning for them to be burglars."

"I wonder who they are," Tony said as he leaned forward.

"How am I supposed to know?" quipped Cecelia. "Why don't you go over and find out?"

Tony looked at his sister and half smiled. He noticed she looked right past him toward the activity next door. A sparkle of anticipation began to play across her face as she slowly began to stand. -

"I bet they have a little girl," she said.

Tony turned and looked toward the movers.

"What do you mean?" he asked.

"It's the girl's furniture that gives it away," replied Cecelia, with a smirk. "That's a girl's dresser, a girl's bed, a girl's vanity. Therefore, I bet they have a little girl!"

"I wonder if she's my age." Cecelia looked directly at Tony and smiled.

Tony shrugged his shoulders.

"She might even be your age, *Father*," laughed Cecelia, pushing Tony's shoulder.

As they stood and watched the trucks unloading, a metallic blue 1957 Chevrolet pulled into the driveway of the house. An attractive middle-aged woman stepped from the driver's side and an equally attractive young girl jumped from the passenger side. They both had long reddish blonde hair that seemed to glisten in the morning sunlight.

"Be careful with my dresser!" the girl shouted to the movers as she got out of the car.

Cecelia stepped back and looked at Tony. He seemed in a trance.

"She does appear to be your age." Cecelia's tone was both cynical and cutting.

Tony only nodded. His acknowledgment was halfhearted. His eyes were riveted on their new neighbors.

"She is cute, isn't she?" remarked Cecelia, smugly.

"Uh huh," said Tony. His voice was barely audible.

"You're off in your own little world, aren't you?" Her words just seemed to flow right past him. "I guess it's just too bad that you won't be able to really be friends with her," said Cecelia as she lightly touched Tony on the shoulder.

Tony suddenly jerked to the side. "What do you mean?"

"You know what I mean."

Tony still looked puzzled as he shook his head. "I really don't."

"Well, she is a girl," smirked Cecelia.

"I can see that!" Tony snapped as he turned to look at the girl once more.

"A priest isn't supposed to have any girlfriends," laughed Cecelia. Cecelia took great care to put emphasis on the word girlfriend.

Tony looked back at his sister, reveling in the brilliance of her own remark. A slight smile played across Tony's lips. "But that doesn't make any difference," he said. "A priest is supposed to be everyone's friend." His voice was solemn and authoritative.

Cecelia turned and looked directly at her brother. She aimed her words at him like fiery darts. "I bet you'd really like to be her friend, wouldn't you?" Her words were caustic. "Plan on hearing her confession, Father?"

"Why are you being so hostile?" asked Tony. "I was only looking at our new neighbors."

"Well, why don't you just go over and introduce yourself to our new neighbors?" she said as she pushed open the door. "They just might want you to bless their new home before they move in!"

Cecelia laughed and darted into the house. Tony just shook his head and returned his attention to next door.

"There's nothing wrong with going over and saying hello," Tony said to himself. "That really would be the right thing to do."

He couldn't seem to take his eyes off the young girl. She really was beautiful. Her long reddish-blond hair almost seemed to match the soft pink glow of her skin. Looking at her, dressed in those blue shorts and white blouse, caused Tony to remember Robert Ryan's words. Robert was a fellow student at the Academy, one of Tony's very close friends. As they walked down the path to the ball field, Robert and Dominic Julianno, Tony's closest friend, had been talking about girls before they all headed home. Robert was describing his encounter with an attractive young lady.

He said he thought he had a 'physical problem', thought Tony. *I asked him if he felt warm and numb inside*. Robert acknowledged that he did. Tony let his eyes dwell on the girl's every movement.

I really didn't know what I was describing, thought Tony, *until this very moment*. Tony's heart quickened as he started down the steps of the porch. He knew that she had seen him. His stomach tightened as he thought about her looking at him.

Beads of sweat formed on the top of his forehead as he tried to regain his composure. The warm, numb feeling in the pit of his stomach continued to grow.

I can't believe what's happening to me, thought Tony. *I think I'm going to be sick.*

When Tony looked up she was there in front of him, as if appearing out of nowhere. Her eyes were deep blue and her face was prettier than any girl he had ever seen. He felt like a dumbfounded idiot just staring at her.

"Hi," she said, smiling, "are you our neighbor?"

Tony swallowed hard and squeezed the rosary in his pocket. He quietly begged God to put words in his mouth. His stomach became tighter and his jaw tightened. As he nodded, he tried desperately to get out the word *yes*.

"Oh, Diane!" called her mother from the house. "I need you to come here a minute."

"I'm coming," she answered. "That's my mom calling and I have to run," she said as she turned and ran off. "By the way, my name's Diane Mott. What's yours?"

"To . . . To . . ." His voice was cracked and broken.

"What?" she yelled back, raising her hand to her ear. "I couldn't hear you."

"TONY! MY NAME IS TONY!" he yelled. His scream was so loud it caused her to stop dead in her tracks. Even the movers stopped and looked at him.

For one split second, which seemed like an eternity, the entire world seemed to completely stand still.

The stunned look on the young girl's face quickly gave way to a shy smile.

"Tony . . . Tony . . . ," she repeated. "That's nice. I'll talk to you later!" She then disappeared through her front door.

Embarrassed, Tony turned to walk away. He felt like an absolute imbecile. At least he hadn't thrown up, and the tightness in his stomach began to loosen. But just as swiftly, he felt the numbness in his body become a tingling sensation.

Oh no, he thought, *I'm going to puke!* It felt as if his stomach had pushed its way into his throat as his breakfast gushed forth.

"There's . . . there's nothing . . . that could be worse than this," he choked as he tried to wipe the mess from his mouth.

As the young seminarian knelt there in the grass, trying to recover from the distress of this mortifying experience, he caught a glimpse of a pair of white sneakers out of the corner of his eye. His eyes then slowly followed the sneakers up past the white socks to the pink skin of Diane's leg. Tony quickly shut his eyes, praying that this was just a dream.

"It's a nightmare. It's got to be a nightmare. This can't be happening."

He turned his head away and opened his eyes, hoping he would find himself in bed just waking up. But his eyes locked, instead, on a second pair of shoes looming before him. The beige slippers covered a familiar pair of feet. He held his hand to block the sun from his eyes as he looked up. The white of Cecelia's teeth appeared brighter than the sunlight itself. Her words even sounded like a thunderous roar.

"Hi, my name's Cecelia," she said in a high-pitched voice. "And this," she said as she pointed directly down to Tony, as if she'd just speared him, "is my soon-to-be-priest brother. His Holiness Tony! What's the matter, Father, did you have too much communion wine?"

It was at that precise moment that Tony wanted the Second Coming to take place!

NINE

As his father pulled into a parking space and got out of the car, it snapped Tony back to reality. But he could still feel a knot forming in his stomach. He swallowed hard and got out of the car to help his father with the bags. He walked around to the trunk.

"Here Dad, let me help you with those."

His voice cracked, but he stiffened up and smiled anyway.

"Are you alright, son?"

"Yeah, I'm fine. I'm just going to miss all of you guys. It just seems like all of this time has gone by so fast."

"I know, for us too. But you'll be back home in no time. When you get back to the Academy, with all your friends, you won't have time to even think about us."

"That's not true and you know it," smiled Tony.

After purchasing the ticket, they learned that the bus would be leaving from terminal eight in about two hours. The cashier also advised them that it should arrive in New York approximately 28 hours after its departure.

"If it stays on schedule," said the cashier while giving Tony's father his change. "I understand that there's a lot of snow up there," he continued, "so it might get there a little later than scheduled."

At terminal eight, the driver was already loading bags into the cargo section of the bus.

"Why don't you go on, Dad," said Tony. "I'll just go ahead and board now and catch up on a little sleep."

Looking a little surprised, he handed the driver Tony's ticket. "I really don't mind staying with you."

"I know," said Tony; "but what are you going to do? Watch me sleep?"

Fred was not a hard man, but he also was not a very affectionate man. So when he looked at Tony with such admiration and then embraced him, Tony was surprised.

"Do you really want to be a priest?" his father asked.

The question took Tony by complete surprise, and his eyes reflected the shock.

"I don't mean that you shouldn't be one," his father explained. "I just want to know if it really is *your* dream."

It took a second for Tony to answer.

"Sure, Dad," he said in an unsure voice. "I know exactly what you mean. I think."

"I'm sorry, son." His father's voice was apologetic. "I didn't mean to start this now, with you getting ready to leave and all. It was a dumb question. Just forget it."

Tony quickly realized that his father was becoming uneasy and frustrated. This was no way for them to part.

"I love you, Dad," he said as he gently reached up and embraced him.

"Same here, son."

Tony had never heard his father tell him that he actually loved him. He knew that he did, but he yearned to hear it, just once. As Tony started to move towards the door of the bus, he stopped momentarily and looked directly into his father's eyes.

"Do you want me to become a priest?"

Now it was his father's turn to be surprised. He uneasily shifted his weight but looked directly at his son.

"It doesn't matter what either I, or your mother, want. The only thing that really matters is what you want."

As Tony slowly boarded the bus and found a seat, he peered through the smoke-colored window. He watched his father step through the double glass doors to go back through the terminal to his car.

I wish I knew what he meant, thought Tony.

He continued to gaze at the tinted glass until he could no longer distinguish his father's figure. He then turned his thoughts to the question his father asked.

"It's not even the question that concerns me," he said to himself. "It's his answer. Or the way he answered. I know he was telling me the truth, but the truth about what?"

"Since you're the only one on board so far," said the driver, "you may as well grab a pillow."

"Thanks," said Tony. "I think I will."

"They're in the compartment right above you. There's also a blanket up there if you need one."

Tony thanked him again and pulled the pillow and blanket from the overhead compartment. He then adjusted his seat and prepared himself for the long and tedious journey to New York City. They would be stopping for lunch in Savannah at approximately one o'clock that afternoon.

It was shortly after the bus pulled out of the terminal that Tony allowed himself to think about the last time he saw Diane Mott. It was at the end of last summer, the summer of 1958. It had been filled with the excitement and joy of adolescence. Although the young seminarian was on a predetermined road to the priesthood, the events of that summer presented a slight detour.

He wanted to stop and smell the roses or, at least, some wild flowers. The most beautiful flower that he had ever seen was Diane Mott. The future-priest knew that he wouldn't stray very far. He also knew that God never intended for him to close his eyes and walk in darkness. Tony knew that God really did want him to view the beauty of His design. And Diane Mott certainly was one of God's beautiful designs.

"I know you're going to become a priest," she said as they walked along the beach on that mid-July afternoon. "I still want us to keep in touch."

"Of course," he said, stopping to face her. "I'm going back to the seminary. Not to prison."

They laughed and hugged each other. Tony froze the moment his flesh touched hers. She felt his body become rigid; his arms seemed to lock in place. A warm summer breeze swirled around them. The scent of the salty air mixed with the sweat of their bodies, arousing their senses. Tony was experiencing an emotion he had never known before. He instinctively pulled her closer, before he realized what he was doing.

"My God!" she gasped, feeling his manhood press hard against her.

"I'm sorry..." His voice cracked. "I'm ... ah ... ah—"

Tony dropped his arms and held them against his side, a half-hearted attempt to pull away. Diane laughed as she pulled him back to her and kissed him gently on the cheek. She could feel his heart racing, the bulge in his bathing suit continuing to grow and becoming even harder.

"It's okay," she whispered softly. "I know you didn't mean anything."

As she slowly moved away from his body, her hand moved along his side, gently up to his chest, and playfully pinched the nipple of his breast. It was now as hard as his manhood.

"You don't look like you're ready for the vow of celibacy," laughed Diane.

Tony's face turned bright red, but his eyes stayed locked on Diane's beautifully freckled body. He could see the mischief in her green eyes as she turned and started to run towards the water.

"Where are you going?" asked Tony.

"To cool off! And I think you should do the same."

"Okay, but wait up," yelled Tony as he broke himself from his trance and started running after her.

"Not on your life!" she yelled.

Diane stopped immediately and turned towards Tony. She then playfully raised her hands as if to ward him off.

"We better keep away from each other," she said as she drew a line in the sand. "You stay on your side of the beach and I'll stay on mine."

She then laughed and ran into an oncoming wave. Diane Mott was unlike any person he had ever known. She was beautiful and exciting. Tony really liked being around her. He liked being around her so much it made him feel guilty. There seemed to be such a fine line between friendship and lust. He was still staring at her when the sudden force of the wave knocked him over. As he lay there he could hear the splashing of her feet as she ran towards him.

"Are you alright?" she yelled, as she got closer.

Her wet body glistened in the sunlight, as she loomed overhead and extended her arm. Tony smiled and raised himself slightly to grab her outstretched hand. The moment they touched, he pretended to slip and started pulling her towards him. The undertow of the outgoing wave loosened her footing. Diane's body came plunging down. Unfortunately, the kneecap of her bent leg was aimed towards Tony's privates. As Tony watched that beautiful knee, attached to Diane's gorgeous leg, coming towards him, he froze in horror. The knee just barely brushed past his once-aroused organ and imbedded itself in the wet sand between Tony's legs.

The terror, excitement, and joy of the moment seemed to swirl through their bodies. They looked deeply into each other's eyes. They kissed. It was the first time that Tony had been kissed by a girl. The kiss was now turning into raw passion. As their bodies began to move closer, a sudden torrent of water pushed them apart.

"I guess God wants you to keep that vow of celibacy!" choked Diane.

"I haven't even taken it yet!" laughed Tony.

"This is Savannah!" the driver announced over the speaker.

Tony was reluctant to allow himself to wake up. His dream about Diane was true, but he kept hoping it would end another way.

What am I saying? He thought. I'm going to be a priest. *How can I possibly entertain these thoughts?* He shook his head and straightened his seat. "I guess I better get some lunch. I still have a long way to go." He then got off the bus and went into the station cafeteria.

TEN

As Tony got on the Staten Island Ferry in September of 1959, he thought about the first time he rode this ferry. It was with the help of a massive black man.

He'd been cold, tired, and wet, and he'd cried all the way to Columbia, South Carolina, from Jacksonville. God had introduced him to an angel. His angel was named Mays Van Williams.

Needing to eat something, Tony had asked the driver if there was enough time to get a meal in the cafeteria.

"Of course," the driver said with a smile. "We'll be here for one hour. That should give you plenty of time to eat and relax."

Almost an hour later, Tony walked out of the cafeteria still depressed. He had eaten a wonderful meal of spaghetti and meatballs—a bittersweet experience, the first meal that he had ever ordered on his own. It was also the first time that he paid for the meal himself. In that moment, he realized fully he could do whatever he wanted. This made him very lonely. He knew no one. His eyes welled up.

When he got back on the bus, he thanked the driver. Just as he was walking back to his seat, tears began to stream uncontrollably down his face. Suddenly a massive black hand reached over Tony's right shoulder and held out a white handkerchief. At first it startled Tony, but when he turned around and saw the gentle smiling face of this huge stranger, he felt a deep sense of calm.

"Is everything okay?" The stranger's voice was thunderous, but warm and soothing.

At first, Tony could only stare at this 6' 5" mountain of a man.

"I'm sorry," Tony answered, reaching for the handkerchief and wiping the tears from his eyes. "It's my first time away from home."

"There's nothing to be ashamed about." The huge black man, dressed in denim overalls and a red flannel shirt, then smiled and bent down in order to look Tony directly in the eyes. He then handed him a piece of peppermint candy, which was wrapped in clear plastic.

"The nice lady in the restaurant, on the colored side," said Mays, "gave it to me in case I gets hungry during the rest of the trip."

Tony looked confused.

"I think," continued Mays, "that right now you probably need this more than me."

Tony nodded, as he returned the handkerchief to this giant of a man.

"That's okay," Mays said. "That's your handkerchief, now."

"What's your name?" Tony asked.

"Mays Van Williams," said the muscular black man as he started to walk past Tony towards the rear of the bus.

"Where are you going Mr. Williams?" Tony asked.

"Where I'm supposed to go," he answered. "The rear of the bus."

"Why?"

"Because it's the law, son."

"But I have an empty seat next to me." Tony had a pleading look in his eyes.

Mays Van Williams stopped and turned towards the young boy. He then squatted low enough to look Tony in the eyes once more. "I knows that's you mean well, son, but they would put me in jail if I sat up here with you."

Tony's eyes widened, and his face depicted his shock. "What!" He said in disbelief. "Then how about if I go back there and sit with you, would they put me in jail?"

"I don't think so," Mays answered in a soft but not very confident voice. "It might be best if you check with the driver, first."

Tony bolted down the aisle way to the front of the bus. Mays could see him talking to the driver. He seemed to talk to him for a long time. After a few minutes, however, Tony turned towards Mays and bolted back to him, but this time he had a huge smile on his face.

"He said it was okay!" Tony blurted out. He then followed Mays to the rear of the bus, where there was an empty seat next to Mays' seat.

"Here," said Mays. "You take the window seat."

"You really don't mind if I sit by the window?"

"Course not," Mays answered with a grin. "Unless you mind sitting next to a colored man."

Confusion spread over Tony's face. "Why would I mind sitting next to a colored person?"

Mays smiled, looking at the pure innocence filling Tony's face.

"You're a breath of fresh air," Mays said, still smiling. "Now what's your name and what is a child like you doing on this bus all alone?"

Tony laughed; it would be easy to be friends with a man like Mays Van Williams. He was a decent man who just plain liked to be nice to people.

Tony and his newfound friend talked into the early hours of the morning. By the time they arrived at the New York Greyhound Bus Station, they knew more about each other than most relatives might.

"I can't believe we're already here," Tony said as he looked out the window.

"Well, it was great meetin' ya, Mister Tony Saleem," said Mays. "You sure did make this trip enjoyable. So, whatcha gonna do now?"

"I guess I need to find out where to get the Staten Island Ferry to get over to the Academy."

"When ya s'posed to be there?" Mays asked.

Tony noticed that Mays' tone had become a little more serious.

"Tomorrow, but I'm sure they won't mind if I came in a day early. Why do you ask?"

"The ferry stopped runnin' 'bout three hours ago. It won't start up till 5:30 in the morning."

"What am I supposed to do?" Tony had a panicked look on his face.

"Don't worry 'bout it none," said Mays, as he put a large hand on the future seminarian's shoulder. "You can stay at my place, with my family and me. It'll be a tight fit, but we'll make it work."

Tony couldn't believe what he was hearing. Mays Van Williams was so kind.

"Are you my guardian angel?" Tony asked.

Mays just shook his head and laughed, then welcoming him into his humble home.

The next morning, Mays Van Williams and his son, Mays Van Williams, Jr., got him to the ferry at 8:00 a.m. Mrs. Van Williams sent them off with a hearty breakfast of ham and eggs, and equally hearty hugs. They promised never to forget each other as Tony hugged Mays and his son goodbye. He then got on the Staten Island Ferry. Tony watched until they were out of sight. The tears then cascaded from his eyes.

When Tony got off the ferry, that day in 1959, unlike the first time he arrived, he hailed a taxi.

When he first arrived on Staten Island in 1957, he decided to walk to the seminary. He still remembered walking nearly a mile, then finally taking a bus for the remaining distance. How sorry people had felt for him when they realized where he was going. He kept asking for directions, and they kept telling him to take a cab. One elderly lady was standing at a bus stop and finally told him to ride with her on the bus. She told him where to get off, which put him less than two blocks from the entrance to the academy.

He also remembered the very first time he saw Augustinian Academy. He just stood there, in the very front of the building, mesmerized by the ominous structure in front of him. He did not notice the man who walked up.

"May I help you?" The voice came from Father John Ferran, the school principal.

"I'm Anthony Saleem," Tony answered, in a startled voice. "I'm new. I mean, I'm just starting here."

It was then that Tony noticed the man wore a long black cassock, gathered at the waist by a dark leather cincture. The garment strangely resembled a nun's habit but for the long black strap which circled his waist and hung along his side from his hip to the floor, giving it a more masculine look.

"Are you a postulant?" Father Ferran asked as he bent down to help the young boy with his suitcase.

"Am I a what?" Tony asked, looking confused but somewhat less scared.

"Are you a new seminarian?" asked Father Ferran. "Are you here to study for the priesthood?"

"Oh yes, I'm here to study to be a priest."

Tony followed Father Ferran inside and got checked in at the registrar's office. Another young postulant then showed him to his room. An imaginative person might call it home away from home, but really what it most resembled was something more ordinary: like a large walk-in closet. Although it resembled a large walk-in closet, it still was perfect in Tony's eyes. This walk-in-closet was a room of his very own, which Tony never had.

ELEVEN

It was hard to believe that he was now sixteen and in his third year. Each year brought him one step closer to his cherished goal of being ordained a priest of the Holy Catholic Church.

His first two years were much regimented and very scheduled. He began each morning just like the one before, with daily Mass followed by breakfast. He would then spend the remainder of the day attending classes. His evenings were also rigorously scheduled with recreational activities followed by dinner. After dinner came evening prayer service, known as Benediction, followed by hours of studying.

The time set aside for studying was known as Magnum Silentium or the "great silence". Once the Magnum Silentium began, no one would be allowed to speak until the next morning. From 8:00 p.m. until 6:00 a.m. Augustinian Academy became a monastery, filled with silent monks.

Monsignor Paul once commented to Tony, during his first year at the academy, that the Magnum Silentium reminded him of his days in Ettal, the Benedictine monastery in Germany, where he was assigned in World War II. He was told by his Archbishop that since he was of German descent, he was the most logical person for that assignment. Italy had allied itself with Germany, which made crossing the border a very simple process. Ettal was also the place from which he barely escaped with his life.

Tony still remembered that conversation as if it happened yesterday, instead of two years ago. It was the intensity of Monsignor Paul's emotions that led Tony to believe every word that came from the elder's mouth.

"I wish you would have been with me," Father Paul said to his freshman seminarian. "Then again, I thank God that you weren't." Father Peter Paul's voice wavered, yet became more impassioned, as he laid out the story to Tony. He described how the Nazis began to gather in large numbers in the city of Munich, about 80 miles northwest of Ettal. The more intense the prior became, the more detailed he became until, in the end, Tony imagined Ettal as the Garden of Eden.

"Dietrich came to me in the early hours of the morning," Father Paul said. "He had a look of total panic as he entered my room. I asked him what was wrong and what had happened. He told me that the Nazis knew about us and what we had done. He then told me that a friend of his from the Abwehr had warned him about a pending raid by the Nazis. They were coming to arrest both him and Dietrich for violating the Fuhrer's specific order against harboring and giving comfort to anyone of the Jewish faith or culture. The Fuhrer himself told the Gestapo that both Dietrich Bonhoeffer and I were to be taken into custody and charged with High Treason. The penalty for such a charge was death by hanging." Monsignor Paul paused to let soak in the impact of his statement.

Without thinking, Tony's words tumbled out. "What happened? Did they kill you?"

Monsignor Peter Paul looked at his young seminarian and burst forth into laughter. Tony hung his head for saying such a stupid thing. The Monsignor looked at Tony, and Tony looked into the Monsignor's eyes. Tony could only see kindness and compassion. Tony and the Monsignor rose from their chairs at the exact same time. It was as if they both knew what the other needed. Tony wrapped his arms around his beloved mentor and the Monsignor was embraced his seminarian.

"I feel so stupid!" Tony said.

"Don't you dare say that about yourself," Father Paul said. His voice and tone were exactly as Tony imagined for Jesus Christ. "You are not stupid, my precious son.

You are so wonderfully and beautifully created by God, and God does not do stupid things. You are emotional, and your heart is on your sleeve and that is what I love the most about you."

As the two slowly released each other, Tony began to laugh. The Monsignor quickly joined him. One of the most vivid of Tony's memories was that of the prior's secretary opening the door to his office, seeing the two of them laughing uncontrollably. She just shook her head and began to laugh as well. She had no idea as to why. She only knew that their laughter brought joy to her heart.

"I'll finish the story tomorrow. I don't think I have the strength to complete it today."

"I understand." Tony began walking out of the prior's office. "I do need to hear, you know. I have to find out if you made it out alive."

Monsignor Peter Paul quickly put his hand over his mouth to hide his smile. He then turned and his whole body shook with delight. Tony quickly left his office and could be heard laughing down the hallway.

"That was such a joyful time," Tony said to himself, the third year of schooling laid out before him as he walked up the stairs to the academy's entrance. "It's been two years and he's never finished the story!"

Tony's eyes welled up as he stepped into the marble hallway of the Academy; he put down his bags and went straight to the prior's office. Monsignor Peter Paul's eyes lit up and his countenance took on a glow as he went to embrace Tony.

"I just had to see you, Monsignor." Tony said. "I was glad to be home, but I truly did miss you."

"I missed you as well. Thank you for the letters and pictures you sent me. They brought back so many happy memories of Our Lady of the Angels. I also intended to ask you to come and see me when you got here. I just gave the request to Father Ferran, so he is either faster than a speeding bullet, or you came here on your own."

Tony smiled and the prior motioned for him to sit down. Immediately the tenor of the moment shifted; Monsignor Paul's face became disturbingly serious. As Tony looked into his eyes he could see that the prior was filled with apprehension.

"What is it?" Tony asked. "What's wrong?"

"What makes you think that anything is wrong?"

"It's your eyes," Tony answered.

"Oh yes," Monsignor Paul smiled as he spoke, gently referencing Tony's beating. "It's that special gift that God gave you after that incident."

"Someday you will tell me about the incident, won't you?" Tony asked.

"God will let us know when the time is right to share that with you."

"I also need for you to finish that story about Ettal. It's been two years and you still have not finished it."

"Oh yes," smiled the prior. "You still want to know if I got out alive!"

Tony smiled and shook his head. "I guess that comment will follow me forever."

"I promise to tell you the rest of that story before I leave." Father Peter Paul's eyes suddenly widened. "I did not mean to say it that way." He seemed very flustered. His face reddened and beads of sweat formed on his forehead.

Tony was frozen in his seat. "What?"

"I did not mean for it to come out that way." He still sounded flustered and embarrassed. "That's also why I wanted to see you. I wanted you to hear it from me and not by way of some rumor."

Tony clasped his hands together and braced himself.

"I had a heart attack, last month." Monsignor Paul let his words sink in. "Although I'm still alive," he laughed as he said the words. Tony also smiled. "I have decided to retire."

Tony breathed a sigh of relief. To not want this man to not retire would be very selfish, Tony realized.

"I know I could not expect you to stay here and take care of me forever, Father. I'm sorry! I mean Monsignor."

Peter Paul laughed. "Tony, as far as I'm concerned, you can call me Peter."

"I like to think of you as my father. I guess that's why I said father."

The Monsignor smiled.

"I know that I can see you sometimes and I can always call you and get your very wise advice. I also know that you'll be there if I really need help." Tony leaned back in his chair as the tears began to flow. "I am so sorry." Tony desperately tried to hold back, and he wiped the tears from his eyes.

Prior Peter Paul stood and came to the young seminarian; he opened his arms. Tony quickly buried his face into his cassock again. He cried and sobbed for the next twenty minutes. The Monsignor just held him and let him know that everything would be all right. Once Tony had gained composure, the Monsignor went on to tell him that he decided to go back to Ettal to retire. He also explained that he would be leaving in the next few days. Father Ferran would be in charge until his replacement arrived.

"Since this is your junior year, I have decided to appoint you as Sacristan," the prior said with a smile. "I have also left explicit orders with Father Ferran to explain our tradition to the new prior."

Tony smiled. The tradition of Augustinian Academy had always been that the Sacristan would be appointed Dean the following year.

"You'll make a wonderful dean."

"I only wish that you could be here and guide me." Tony's voice cracked.

"God will always be with you, and I can assure you that he will guide you. Just remember to do the right thing and you will always be in God's will."

The Monsignor embraced Tony once more. "Come back tomorrow and I'll finish that story for you."

"I will." Tony nodded.

TWELVE

Tony made his way to the third floor. He still remembered how difficult it was to walk those steps when he first arrived. He also remembered carrying that fifty-pound footlocker up three flights. He was only carrying two suitcases this time, but for some reason it seemed more difficult this time.

"I bet you wish I was helping you again." It was the unmistaken voice of Dominick Julianno.

"Dom, you're here. Did you decide to come in early, or did your dad finally kick you out?" laughed Tony.

"That's cute. Real cute." Dominick immediately wrapped his arms around Tony.

Tony still remembered the first time he met his closest friend. It was on those same steps. Tony was struggling with his foot locker and a suitcase, attempting to get them both up the three flights to his room. Dominick had just gotten there. His bags were being carried for him by his chauffer.

"Hold on!" Dominick yelled to Tony. "Let me help you with that." He then took Tony's suitcase from his hand and set it aside at the bottom of the first level.

"What are you doing?" asked Tony. "That my suitcase."

"I know," said Dom. "Reggie will get it after he puts my stuff away. You and I can get this thing." He lifted the other end of the footlocker.

Tony just smiled. It was the beginning of the closest friendship that he ever had. When it was too expensive for him to go home during holidays like Thanksgiving, he spent it with the Julianno family. They literally were his second family.

Dominick's father, Joseph Julianno, was one of the top legal minds in all of the New York. In fact, he was reputed to be the best lawyer in the nation. He was also reputed to be the "Consigliore", the legal counselor, for the Gambino crime family. In the early part of their friendship Dominick would vehemently deny this. After Tony had become so close to the family, however, Joseph himself told Tony that he was part of the Gambino crime family.

It was an overt act which depicted the closeness of the bond that Tony shared with the Juliannos.

"Come on!" said Dom as he ran down the corridor, carrying one of Tony's suitcases.

"Why are you in such a hurry? We just got here. Nothing could be that urgent."

"Oh yes, it could," Dom yelled over his shoulder, still running.

"Congratulations!" said Dominick when Tony caught up to him.

"For what?" asked Tony, as he opened the door for his new room.

"First of all, because you got a corner room."

"We all get new rooms, Dom," smiled Tony. "Remember we're juniors. We move to a different wing in the Academy. We have to make room for incoming freshmen. We do it every year."

"Yeah, but yours is a corner room!" snapped Dom, as he pushed open the door.

"What's so special about a corner room?" Tony looked puzzled.

"Oh, I guess it could be a mistake." Dom smiled knowingly.

"Come on, Dom!" demanded Tony. "It's been a long trip. I just got here. I've got to get moved in. Gimme a break! What's this all about?"

"All right," said Dom. "Do you know whose room this was last year?"

Tony looked around the completely stripped room, with its bare walls and frugal furnishings.

"They all look alike, Dom," Tony mumbled.

He backed up and stepped out of the room. The handwritten name *WALSH* was still on a piece of tape on the right side of the doorframe. Tony's face lit up.

"This was Sean's old room!" he said, surprised.

"That's right!" shouted Dominick.

"That doesn't mean anything. Other than I got lucky, and got the sacristan's old room."

"You mean the former sacristan! Don't you?"

"That's right," said Tony. "Everyone is speculating that he'll be the new dean."

"Well the speculation is over," said Dom. "He's already been appointed."

"That's great," acknowledged Tony. "I really do like Sean, but what does this have to do with my room?"

"You really don't know anything, do you?" smirked Dom. "You really have to understand the politics of this Academy if you intend to become dean someday."

"Okay, Monsignor Ambassador! Just what are the politics of Augustinian Academy?" A smile played across Tony's lips. He was enjoying this so much. Monsignor Paul had already told him that he appointed Tony as the sacristan, with the hopes of him becoming dean. Tony, however, did not want to break the Monsignor's trust. Besides, he was also enjoying Dominick's drama very much.

Dominick held up the crumpled piece of carbon paper. He then slid his hand beneath the front of his cassock and pulled a neatly folded sheet of paper from his shirt pocket.

"What's that?"

"It's the answer to all of your political dreams," answered Dominick. His grin strongly resembled that of an Italian Cheshire cat.

"What makes you think I've got any political dreams?" Tony said as he reached for the paper.

"Don't be so hasty. I have to explain it to you," Dominick said, then handed Tony the crumpled piece of carbon paper. "Open that up," explained Dominick, "and follow along."

Tony stretched out the carbon and held it up to the light.

"As you can see," Dominick continued, "that's a carbon of the official room listings."

Tony nodded. "But how did you get this?"

"Let's just say I accidently saw it in the trash can when I went to the principal's office to get my room key. No one was there."

Tony's eyes rolled as he shook his head.

"How I got it, however, is not all that important. It is obviously an official Academy listing."

"You're right. I'm sorry I asked."

"Can we continue now?"

Tony nodded.

"The one thing about this list, however," Dominick's voice began to deepen with authority. "Is that it also shows each person's duty and responsibility for the prospective year."

Tony quickly began to search for his name.

"Don't strain yourself too much," smiled Dominick, feeling that he had Tony in the palm of his hand. "I've transcribed all of it for you. I know how difficult it is to read that carbon paper."

Dominick then handed Tony the neatly folded piece of paper. "Just remember this when you become dean," he mocked.

Tony shook his head as he opened the paper.

"Sacristan!" Tony blurted out. "I'm actually going to be the sacristan!" Tony surprised himself, as to how surprised he could act.

"That's right, your holiness!" Dominick taunted. "Are you going to make me genuflect each time I pass in front of you?"

"Knock it off!" Tony laughed. "This really is quite an honor."

"I know," said Dominick, grabbing Tony by the shoulder. "It's the job Sean Walsh had before he became dean and John McCarthy before him."

"Maurice Murphy was also the Academy sacristan!" Tony chimed in.

"Yeah," said Dom, looking very thoughtful. "Maurice was dean the year I saved your life from having a heart attack bringing in your overweight footlocker."

Tony immediately cut his eyes towards Dom and smiled. Dom was truly a dear and close friend, thought Tony.

All he could do was embrace Dominick and say, "Thank you. You know you'll always be the closest friend I've got," said Tony as tears welled up in his eyes.

"Don't get mushy on me," laughed Dom. "We still have politics to take care of."

"You know, you may be right," said Tony, as he pushed away from Dom and put both hands on his shoulders. "There might be something to this."

"Now you're catching on," Dominick said, grabbing both of Tony's shoulders in turn. "As I said earlier, congratulations!"

Tony just smiled. He knew that this would be a year that he would never forget. He also had an ominous feeling that it would be a year that would have its most demanding challenges.

THIRTEEN

"BENEDECAMUS DOMINO!"

"DEO GRATIAS!"

The usual morning ritual had begun. The sharp rap at the door. The giving of praises to the Lord and thanks to God. The reluctant rising to a cold morning. It was becoming all too familiar.

Tony had adjusted to his return to the seminary quicker than he had hoped. It was as if he wanted to be here as much as, if not more than, home. He was becoming comfortable with his new lifestyle and he felt guilty. Only a few days had passed since Tony's return to the hill and already his thoughts about home were quickly fading into a simple memory.

"Did you hear anything about the prior leaving?" asked Dominick.

Tony stopped walking and turned to his friend. The cold night air whistled through the open courtyard and caused Tony's cheeks to become numb.

"Well?" asked Dom again.

"What do you mean?" asked Tony.

"Are you alright?" asked Dom, "You're acting kind of strange."

"I'm sorry," Tony answered, "I guess I wasn't listening to you."

"I know that you're real close to him, so I figured you'd know."

Tony nodded. "He is leaving, Dom. He's going back to Ettal, in Germany."

"Why? Isn't he happy here?"

"Of course he is. He had a heart attack. I guess the stress of this place is too much for him."

"That makes sense." Dominick nodded.

"What makes sense?" asked Robert Ryan as he walked towards Tony and Dominick.

"Can you believe this?" Dominick looked at Tony and they both started laughing.

Robert was wearing his black cassock, tied with a cincture, but then paired with a red baseball cap covering a pair of hot-pink fluffy earmuffs.

"Robert, you never cease to surprise me," Tony said as he continued to laugh.

"Why?" Robert asked, in total innocence. "All I asked was what makes sense? How is that funny?"

Tony thought about the many times that Robert amazed even the most cynical of students with his pure innocence and naiveté—like that walk to the ball field during their freshman year.

When the scheduled classes would end for the day, the "day-hops" would go home and the postulants would prepare for their afternoon recreational activity. As Tony and Dom were walking along the path leading to the softball field, they could hear Robert coming up behind them.

"Hey, wait up, guys," yelled Robert from behind them, "I need to ask you something."

Tony and Dom slowed down and waited for Robert to catch up.

"No. Whatever the question is, the answer is no," Dom said, as soon as Robert caught up to them. "I'm not going to lend you anymore money and I won't let you ride in my dad's limo, and I'm not going to will you my mink-lined Roman collar when I die."

"Knock it off! I have something serious to ask you," Robert said.

"So do I," Tony said, as he turned towards Dom. "How is it you have a mink-lined Roman collar and I didn't know about it? Me. Your best friend. I'm crushed. You don't trust me."

"It's a family heirloom. My grandfather was a priest."

"Oh, well that's different. That certainly explains everything. Go ahead, Robert, ask us your burning question."

"Have you guys ever ... Wait a minute?" Robert stopped in mid-sentence. There was a long pause. He then turned towards Dominick.

"How could your grandfather be a priest?"

Both Tony and Dom began laughing at the same time, in spite of their valiant attempt to keep the joke running.

"Ok, good joke! You got me this time but I really do have a serious question for you guys."

"Fire away," said Tony.

"Do you guys ever think about girls?" Robert asked very seriously.

They both stared at Robert for a full minute.

"What do you mean?" Tony asked.

"Why would you ask us a question like that?" Dom chimed in.

Robert kept looking down at the ground as they continued to walk towards the softball field. It became deathly silent. Suddenly, Tony stopped walking and put his hand on Robert's shoulder.

"You're serious, aren't you?"

Robert would not look up from the path. His eyes were glued to the concrete path and his face was a bright red.

"I think something's wrong with me," Robert said, still looking down. "Lately, I've been thinking a lot about girls. I also might have a physical problem but I don't know what it is."

"What kind of physical problem?" asked Dom, in a sympathetic voice, which was totally out of character. "Do you feel sick to your stomach or something?"

"No," interrupted Tony. "I think I know what he means."

Robert looked up and quickly cut his eyes towards Tony. "You do?"

"Do you feel kind of warm and numb inside?"

Robert eyes began to widen, as he nodded vigorously.

"Do you also feel like something inside you wants to burst open?"

By this time, Robert was looking directly at Tony. He continued to nod his head in agreement. He was hanging on his every word. Robert's jaw began to drop as he anticipated Tony's final statement.

"And you feel 'hard'."

"That's it!" Robert exclaimed. His words seemed to burst forth uncontrollably at this point. "My nooney gets hard. It gets hard as a rock!"

At that very instant Robert realized what he had said. His face turned red as a beet and droplets of sweat began to form on his forehead. The embarrassment was overwhelming.

Dominick's reaction was instinctive.

"Your *nooney?*" he asked Robert with uncontrollable laughter. "Is that . . . Is that?" Dom began to grasp his stomach with his arms and double over with hysterical laughter. "Is that what you call it? A *nooney?*"

By now tears were rolling across Dom's cheeks. He lay on the ground and kicked his feet in the air, trying to control his laughter.

"Is ... is that . . . is that . . ." Dom could hardly talk from laughing so hard. "Is that what you wee wee with?"

Robert was devastated. Tears also began to roll down his cheeks. His, however, were tears of humiliation.

"Stop it!" Tony snapped at Dom. "Stop laughing and get off the ground. This isn't funny."

It was difficult for Tony to maintain his composure with Dominick sprawled on the ground, kicking and screaming and looking an awful lot like a turtle on its back trying desperately to right itself.

"I'm sorry," Tony tried to console Robert. "I understand how you must feel. Obviously, Dom doesn't. Don't pay any attention to him."

Robert turned away and started walking towards the softball field.

"Robert! Wait," Tony yelled after him, trying to control the contagious effect of Dominick's continuous laughter. "We'll talk about this later. That is, if you want to?"

Robert, not sure of the sincerely of Tony's offer, just glanced over his shoulder at Tony and nodded as he continued to walk towards the field.

It was the next day that brought out the truly naïve Robert. It also gave a clearer picture of the character and integrity of Father John Ferran.

FOURTEEN

"The male genitals . . ."

Father Ferran's voice seemed different, as he described the human reproductive system on that Friday morning. His voice was deeper, more resonant, and more authoritative.

"A man, or boy," continued Father Ferran, "has a finger-shaped organ in the pubic area of his body, which is between his legs."

Father Ferran then turned away from the board and faced the class.

"What is that organ called?" he asked the class.

Dominick's hand immediately shot up. "Alright," said Father Ferran, as he pointed to Dom. "Julianno, you seem to be very anxious to answer this question. So, go ahead and tell us."

As Dominick stood up to answer the question, he turned and looked directly at Robert, who was seated on his left. "Since we studied these chapters together, I hope that Robert will correct me if I mispronounce the word."

By now the entire class had heard about the Robert Ryan "nooney" incident. Dominick Julianno's ability to disseminate gossip was equal only to that of a national slander magazine.

The anticipation of the class was so great that Father Ferran even noticed the tension.

"Julianno!" said Father Ferran, very sternly. "You don't have to give an editorial commentary. Just answer the question."

Robert's face looked pale and drawn as the muscles in his jaw began to tighten. He gripped the table so tightly that his knuckles began to turn white. A slight smile played across Dominick's lips as he cut his eyes away from his tormented friend.

"PENIS!" shouted Dominick as he looked directly at Father Ferran. "It's called a penis."

A puzzled look spread across Father Ferran's face, as he squinted his steel-blue eyes. The tense atmosphere in the room began to slowly dissipate as Robert breathed a sigh of relief.

"That's correct," Father Ferran said. "The correct biological name of that organ is penis."

Father Ferran's movements were slow and deliberate as he began to walk towards the table at which Robert was seated.

"There is a small sack which hangs behind the penis," he continued, "and this is called the scrotum."

Robert could feel the harsh disciplinarian's ominous presence directly in front of him. He kept his eyes glued to his notebook and refused to look up.

"The scrotum contains two oval-shaped sex organs," Father Ferran's thunderous voice seemed to pound its way into Robert's ears as the priest leaned forward and gently touched the top of the young seminarian's head. "And what are they called?" snapped the teacher.

Robert's eyes widened as his head jerked up, and he found himself looking directly into the steel-blue eyes of his science teacher. His answer would set into motion a series of statements that would mark him for life.

"Balls!" The word spun from Robert's mouth, almost detached.

The absolute shock of Robert's answer shrouded the room with a deadly silence. This lasted about two seconds. Then the entire class exploded with laughter.

"My God!" said Robert. Tears welled in his eyes. His face resembled a contorted beat.

Father Ferran's entire face seemed to tighten as he loomed over the visibly shaken postulant. Tony over and bit his lip to keep from laughing. He did not want to turn the attention and wrath of the priest towards him.

"I'm sorry, Father! I'm so sorry." Robert's voice began to crack. "I ... re... I really ... am sorry, Father. I hope you ... and God ... will forgive me."

Robert's face was covered with tears as he buried it in his arms against the top of the table. But he continued to babble.

"I don't know what I'm saying. Please ... Please ... Don't kill me!" Robert slowly lifted his head.

Tony caught a glimpse of Robert's face out of the corner of his eye. Tears were rolling down the left side of Robert's cheek.

"I really didn't know!" continued Ryan. His voice was broken and confused. "I thought that Dom..."

Father Ferran leaned forward. He was only a few inches from the distraught postulant's face.

"You thought that Dom, what?" whispered the harsh disciplinarian.

"I thought that Dom…" Ryan's voice began to squeak, as he tried to hold back the sobs. His pause, however, was not long enough. An eternity would not have been long enough.

"I really thought he was going to say NOONEY!"

Robert's words caused the class, already exploding with laughter, to erupt like a volcano. Tony jolted backwards, sitting straight up in his seat. He then looked at Robert in total disbelief. Tony's sudden movement caused Father Ferran to look directly at him. The priest's cold steel-blue eyes generated within Tony a strange feeling. Father Ferran's gaze was trance-like, and its intensity seemed to burn into Tony's soul. He was held captive by what he saw.

They were the eyes of a holy man, but one who had a deep secret.

"Why do you stare so intently?" asked the priest. His voice was calm and deliberate.

"I'm sorry," said Tony, jerking away, "I was just shocked by Robert's answer."

The priest only nodded. He then slowly turned and walked towards the front of the room. As Father Ferran wrote the words TESTICLES OR TESTES on the board, the room once again became coldly silent.

"The testicles consist of a complicated system of tubes," said Father Ferran. His voice was firm and convincing. He acted as if nothing had happened. "Millions of sperm are produced and stored within these tubes," he continued, "a tube called the vas deferens carries sperm from each testicle to a tube called the urethra…."

As Father Ferran went on to describe the entire male reproductive system, the entire class took very detailed notes. Dom, however, would periodically raise his head and glance at Robert. Each time he did so, a sympathetic smile would play across his lips.

Robert's humiliation was so great that he kept his eyes glued to his paper.

"All female reproductive organs," said the priest, "are inside of the female's body...."

Robert looked up quickly to copy the word "vulva" that Father Ferran had written on the board.

"The vulva," said the teacher, "is a hood-like structure which is comprised of small folds of skin. It is located between the female's legs." Father Ferran then turned from the board and looked towards the class. "The vulva covers the opening to a narrow canal, which is known as what?"

When he asked the question, he was looking directly at Robert. Dom bit his lip and Tony gripped his pencil so hard that it broke in his hand. Robert's face became a pale white and sweat formed across the top of his lip.

"Don't worry, Mr. Ryan," said the priest, "I wouldn't dare ask you for the answer." His voice was cold and monotone. "I would be afraid that I might get an answer like NOOKY, or some other similar term!"

The class couldn't believe what they had just heard. Father John Ferran was not a humorous man. He would seldom even have a smile on his face. He was cold and stern. In spite of the fact that he was a priest, he still represented the highest form of discipline. The word was so out of character for him that it left the class stunned. Everyone sat in silence, without even the slightest hint of laughter. It wasn't until Robert spoke that the students put the comment into its proper perspective.

"Then what's it really called?" blurted out Robert.

The wave of laughter which filled the room caused the priest to simply shake his head. It was as if he was doing all he could to keep from smiling.

"Vagina," said the priest. "The word, Mr. Ryan, is vagina. It's a penetrating word. So, please try to remember it."

Very few caught his humor.

The bell rang sharply.

"Class dismissed," Father Ferran said, still shaking his head.

FIFTEEN

"We were just talking about the prior leaving," Dominick said to Robert. "The fact that he had a heart attack and is going to live in Ettal is what makes sense."

Robert's jaw dropped, and his arms fell to his side. He appeared to be in a daze. It was the first time since he met them that either Tony or Dominick had ever actually answered one of his questions or concerns.

"You are actually telling me the truth, aren't you?" Robert said in a somewhat stunned but monotone voice.

"Of course we are," answered Tony. "He's leaving in three days. There's going to be a retirement party for him tomorrow."

"Everyone is supposed to be here," Dominick chimed in. "The bishop is coming, as well as the archbishop. I also hear that Cardinal Spellman will be here."

"Cardinal Spellman! You're kidding!" Robert said.

"You're right. I am kidding," Dominick said with a smile.

The sharp sound of the bell brought an abrupt end to their conversation. They had only ten minutes to get to their rooms before the next bell would sound. This would signify the beginning of their scheduled study period. Exactly two hours later, the bell would ring again to announce the end of the study period, and the beginning of the *Magnum Silentium*. The seminarians would then have exactly thirty minutes to prepare for bed. This would have to be done in complete silence since it was the *Magnum Silentium*

Everyone was strictly held to this schedule except for Tony. One of the joys of being the sacristan was the fact that he could use some of this time to make things ready for the next morning's worship services. He would make sure that the hymnals were out and the priest's vestments were properly prepared. It was also his responsibility to insure that the cruets, small flat-bottomed vessels with narrow necks that held the wine and water, were in place and ready to be filled in the morning.

The final bell, marking the beginning of lights out, sounded just as the newly-appointed sacristan had completed his evening responsibilities. He turned out the lights in the sanctuary and chapel and slowly made his way to his room. His shoes made a soft tapping sound down the hallway. The sound reminded him of the times he heard Sean Walsh's feet make that same sound after lights out. He thought about how jealous he'd been. He then smiled; he had achieved one of his dreams. He was now the sacristan.

As Tony stepped into his corner room, his happiness and joy were suddenly shrouded. He looked at the statue of the Mother Mary sitting on the top of his dresser. It was the one that his mother and father had given him for Christmas. His heart skipped a beat as he undressed and climbed into bed. His mind flew back to that early Christmas morning.

"Tony, Tony get up", whispered Johnny as he shook his big brother by the shoulder.

In a state of half consciousness and half sleep, Tony answered, "Deo Gratias, Deo Gratias!"

"What? Get up, it's Christmas. Let's go look under the tree!"

Johnny pulled Tony by the arm, trying to drag him out of bed.

"Oh man, what time is it? It's still dark outside," said Tony.

Then the future priest's eyes met the face of the lit electric clock on his nightstand.

"It's five-thirty! Are you crazy? Go back to bed and leave me alone. Come back at 7:00. Now that is at least a decent hour to get up."

"Aw, come on Tony, Santa's already been here and I can't sleep anyway. Please get up with me. I can't wait. Let's go get Cecelia. Hurry up!"

This ritual had been going on in the Saleem home for as long as Tony could remember. The youngest would inevitably wake up first, and then go get the other two older kids. When all three were up, they would sneak into the living room and take a look at the Christmas tree overflowing with Christmas presents.

The children would sit under the tree and begin opening their presents, trying to be as quiet as possible, but this didn't last too long. When the presents had been opened amid laughter and talking about what each had gotten, Ophelia came into the room, wearing her traditional Christmas robe of red velvet with lace and green ribbons, and would turn on the lights.

"You need to be quiet in here," she would say with a smile. "Your father is still trying to sleep."

She went through the living room and into the kitchen and poured herself a cup of coffee and went back to the living room to watch her children revel in their joy. It was very evident that she loved Christmas and the joy and laughter it brought to her home.

Christmas morning at the Saleem house was usually very predictable, but this Christmas seemed different to Tony, somehow. He felt like he was a visitor instead of a member of the family.

"Do you like it?" his mother asked.

"Yes… Of course," said Tony. "It's beautiful," he replied with as much enthusiasm as he could muster.

His squirming actions and looks of confusion, however, betrayed his words.

"Your father and I got it from the church," she said proudly.

"You stole it from the church!" Johnny said, in shock.

"Of course not!" snapped his mother. "We bought it at the church sanctuary sale. It was very expensive."

"It's perfect, Mom," Tony said politely as he lifted the statue to the light.

"What is it?" asked Johnny.

"It's the Virgin Mary and the Christ Child," answered his mother. "When you become a priest, you can put it in your church and everyone will know how much your parents love you and how proud they are of you."

His mother's face glowed as bright as the statue's as she leaned over to touch it.

"But suppose he doesn't become a priest?" Retaliated Cecelia in her usual sarcastic tone.

The words spewed from Ophelia's mouth like venom from a snake. "Shut your damned mouth, and don't ever say that again!"

All three children sat frozen. Her entire body seemed to convulse as she snatched the statue from Tony's hand and held it directly in front of Cecelia.

"YOU LOOK AT THIS, YOU HARLOT!"

Cecelia's frightened eyes became wide and lifeless as tears streamed down her pale ghost-like face.

"HE WILL BECOME A PRIEST!" She continued to scream and shake uncontrollably. "THEN YOU AND YOUR DAMNED BROTHERS WILL HAVE TO GO TO HIM TO GET FORGIVENESS FOR YOUR SINS!"

"Ophelia! *Laht!*"

The voice above their mother's head was authoritative and cold, sounding *"Laht"* in a way that only their father could speak it. It was an Arabic slang term which literally meant "No!" It translated, however, into the emphatic command: "Stop it! And get a grip on yourself!"

Fred rarely raised his voice, much less raised it to his wife, in front of his own children. Tony, shocked, remembered the time, many years prior, when he raised his own voice to his mother and his father made him literally kiss her feet.

This can't be the same man, thought Tony. *There's something wrong here. And this absolutely can't be the same woman.*

Fred's deep brown eyes were cold, but firm, as he stared at his wife and motioned towards the bedroom. Ophelia hesitated for only a second, before the realization of what she had done engulfed her.

"Oh... My... God!" She fell to her knees and began to rock back and forth as she shook and sobbed uncontrollably.

When her husband bent down to pick her up, she jerked her head back and unleashed a wail, which resembled that of a wounded animal.

"What's wrong with Emma?" screamed Johnny. He reverted to the Lebanese language only when he was scared. Really scared.

"Nothing!" snapped his father. "I'll take care of it. Just go back to opening your presents."

As he led her into the bedroom, he glanced back at Tony. His eyes locked on to Tony's frozen gaze.

Chills ran down Tony's spine. He sat there staring into the eyes of his father. At that very moment, his gift was once again validated. In that flash of a second Tony knew that his father was burdened with a secret. A secret that filled his father with both terror and guilt.

Tony instantly cowered back in fear, pulling away from his father's gaze. His life would never be the same.

He sat up with a start. He was covered in sweat on that cold September morning. He remembered seeing the same look in his father's eyes as he was leaving to come back. It was when his father asked him if he really wanted to be a priest.

SIXTEEN

The retirement celebration for Monsignor Peter Paul was beyond description. The Ladies of Mother Mary, the mothers of all of the students who attended Augustinian Academy, had cooked all of the food and decorated the main auditorium and cafeteria for the occasion. It was probably the most opulent setting that anyone had ever seen or experienced. It was a tribute to this beloved prior, who had been there only for the past three years.

Monsignor Paul was overwhelmed and brought to tears on several occasions. Tony was beaming with pride when the prior asked him to sit next to him during the celebratory dinner. The dinner, however, was interrupted when Father John Ferran walked up to the table and announced that there were a few guests entering the dining room at that time. The first one to enter was Fulton J. Sheen, the Auxiliary Bishop and the Archbishop of the New York. The second to enter was Terence James Cooke, the secretary to Cardinal Francis J. Spellman. Everyone stood and greeted them with applause.

They both came and joined the Monsignor at the head table. Monsignor Paul was introducing them to Tony when Secretary Cooke stopped him in mid-introduction. "We have already heard so much about you, Tony," he said, smiling. "It is as if we already know you."

"Thank you, your eminence," Tony said, blushing.

"No, no," laughed Secretary Terrance Cooke. "You call the next person you are going to meet *your eminence* not me."

It was at that moment that Tony saw the Monsignor look past him with a look of total surprise.

"Your Eminence," the Monsignor's voice was filled with shock.

Tony turned around and stared into the face of Cardinal Francis Joseph Spellman.

"My God!" said Tony as he dropped to one knee to kiss the Cardinal's ring.

Cardinal Spellman laughed as he lifted Tony to his feet. "I am definitely not Him. I am only a man. I am also way too short to be Him." The hall erupted with laughter.

"I suppose you're talking about that nasty incident with FDR when he was Secretary of the Navy," Monsignor Paul quipped.

"That is exactly right!" laughed the Cardinal. "He said I was too short and then he was the one who appointed me as the Apostolic Vicar for the US Armed Forces. I never could understand that man."

The Cardinal then turned to Monsignor Peter Paul and held out his hand to him. "The one who truly has all of our respect is this man of God," he said as he embraced Monsignor Peter J. Paul, kissing him on both cheeks.

"I did not mean to interrupt this wonderful celebration and meal, but I did come with a purpose," the Cardinal said. He then motioned for everyone to have a seat. "I am not here to take over these festivities, but I do have an important announcement." He then motioned to his Secretary Terrance Cooke to bring in the surprise. The Cardinal was then handed a large manila envelope, which was sealed. He handed the envelope to Monsignor Peter Paul.

The Monsignor took the envelope and looked at the address, as well as the return address. The papal seal was embossed on the back. His hands began to tremble and tears began to flow down his cheeks. He slowly handed the entire envelope to Tony.

"Help me," he said. "Please open it for me."

"Of course," said Tony, whose hands were also shaking. He opened the package and pulled out a parchment written in Latin. As he started to hand the parchment back, Monsignor Peter Paul stopped him and asked him to please read it out loud. Tony nodded and began to read it in Latin.

The Cardinal touched Tony on the shoulder.

"I think he wants you to translate it," Cardinal Spellman said.

Tony's face turned a bright red. "He must have more faith in my Latin than I do."

The entire table broke out into laughter.

"Yes I do," acknowledged the Monsignor.

Tony translated:

To my dear and beloved friend, Peter J. Paul. I wish I could be there to celebrate your well-deserved retirement today, but my health would not permit me to make the trip at this time. I wanted you to know, however, that your leadership and expertise will be greatly missed at Augustinian Academy. You remain and always will be an inspiration to all of us. Your courage and determination in the face of overwhelming odds during the war has not only been an encourage-ment to us all, but also, it has set a new standard for integrity.

Tony looked at the Monsignor; tears flowed freely down his cheeks. Cardinal Spellman just nodded and motioned for Tony to continue. "You are the one he wants to read this," the Cardinal said.

Peter Paul handed Tony a handkerchief.

"It is for this reason," Tony continued, *"that I am honored..."* Tony's eyes widened and his heart seemed to skip a beat. *"That I am honored at the recommendation of Cardinal Francis Joseph Spellman of the Archdiocese of New York, to elevate you to the position of Bishop of the Holy Catholic Church."*

Tony looked at the joyful expression on the new Bishop's face. "It is signed by His holiness, John the Twenty Third." Tony said. "I have never seen his signature before, but I'm sure this is it."

The hall erupted into laughter. Cardinal Spellman immediately motioned Cooke. A large box made of red velvet was brought in. The Cardinal opened it and removed the Bishop's hat and a jeweled cross. He handed the hat to now Bishop Peter J. Paul, and he handed the cross on a pillow to Tony to present to the Bishop.

The young seminarian was so overwhelmed that his tears flowed freely. Bishop Paul set the pillow and cross on the table and embraced Tony. They both wept. The hall erupted in applause as everyone came to their feet. There was not a dry eye in the place. Even Cardinal Spellman let the tears run down his cheeks.

Tony was nearly brought to tears again when the Monsignor was giving his farewell speech. He thanked everyone, especially the Cardinal and the Auxiliary Bishop Fulton Sheen, Terrance Cooke, and Cardinal Spellman. He repeated how overwhelmed he was with the papal letter and surprise promotion.

"I guess the Pope figures that since I'm retired then I really can't do much to screw it up."

Everyone was brought to their feet once more with joyous laughter.

"I will miss all of you so very much," he continued. "I will especially miss my dear student, postulant, and friend from my parish in Jacksonville, Florida, Tony Saleem." He then pointed directly at Tony.

The cafeteria exploded with applause. Tony could see that the one applauding the loudest was Dominick Julianno.

It was almost midnight when the festivities finally came to a close. The Bishop asked Tony to walk with him for a minute. "I realized that I had not finished telling you the end of that story," he said. "I also realize that time will not allow me to finish it before I leave."

The look of disappointment crossed Tony's face, but he was determined to not dampen this bright and beautiful time for the new Bishop.

"Monsignor. I mean Bishop—" Tony's face reddened. "What I really mean is *father*. You are a father to me." The tears came again. "I will miss you so much. I don't know what…"

The Bishop pulled Tony to him. "There is no need to say anything else," he softly said. "I will write you and tell you everything, my son. You truly are like a son to me." He continued to hold him and they both wept once more.

SEVENTEEN

Bishop Peter J. Paul's retirement was the talk of all of Staten Island and most of New York for weeks to come. Father Ferran stated very openly that he would have some very large shoes to fill for the next few weeks because it was decided by Cardinal Spellman not to name a replacement for Bishop Paul until after the Thanksgiving Holiday. In the meantime Cardinal Spellman named Father Ferran as the acting prior.

The question which kept going through the school was who the new prior would be? Many felt that Father Ferran should be given the position. Tony's feelings about the matter, however, were cut short by something else—the Thanksgiving holidays would be spent with the Julianno family. This had become a tradition for Tony.

The excitement of the upcoming Thanksgiving holidays seemed to electrify every seminarian, from the freshmen to the seniors—but perhaps Tony most of all. Still, he grew anxious as it dawned on him—he was more excited by the thought of Thanksgiving with the Juliannos than of Christmas with his own family.

Their ride from Staten Island to Dominick's home in Long Island was long, but made in the lap of luxury. It was one of the most enjoyable and exciting trips that Tony had ever had. Although Dominick had ridden in a limousine many times over, he shared in Tony's joy. It was no different this time.

The night before Thanksgiving had given new life to New York City. Ornaments and lights were strung everywhere in preparation for the upcoming Christmas holidays. It looked more like Christmas than Thanksgiving. The sights, the sounds, the excitement, he drank it all in with an insatiable thirst. There really was no place like New York for the holidays!

"Don't you ever get the desire to just move up here?" Dominick asked.

"Not really," Tony answered, though loving the festivities fully. "It still seems too big and too crowded."

"I think that you should enlighten your mind and someday move to the most cultured city in the world."

As the limousine drove through the huge wrought iron gates and around the circular drive of the Julianno home, Tony remember how amazed he was the first time he saw it. He still remembered how he stared at the huge mansion and whispered,

"You live here?"

Dominick's answer was a classic.

"No, stupid," laughed Dominick. "I'm visiting! Of course I live here! I have a mom and a dad and two brothers and one dumb sister who also live here."

Tony looked over at his dearest friend. "This place is still huge, Dom."

Dominick laughed. "I still remember. There's my dad. I'm sure he wants to see you more than me."

Joseph was standing there in a sweater and dark pants. His wife Maria beamed as she locked eyes with the two boys.

"Thank you, Lambert," she yelled to the driver, "for bringing them home safely once again."

"It was absolutely my pleasure, Mrs. Maria," Lambert answered. He looked much older this year. His hair was still white but there was much less of it. He had talked very seriously of retiring before, or just after, Christmas.

This particular Thanksgiving at the Julianno house was one of the best that Tony could remember. The Julianno family always did their best to make him feel as if he were part of their own family; but this year he actually felt like he was part of their family.

Dominick's father, Joseph, was like a character from central casting. One could easily see why he was one of New York's more prominent attorneys. What was not evident to Tony, however, was the fact that this articulate and impeccably mannered father of four was part of the most powerful organized crime families in New York.

His quick wit and personality could captivate any jury. His warm smile could disarm the coldest heart. It was his knowledge of the law, however, that catapulted him to the peak of success.

Joseph Julianno had three primary passions. They were money, respect, and the history of Europe, especially during World War II. It was his passion for European history, however, that most captivated him, causing him to literally turn his basement into a private movie theater. This was his own private sanctuary. He could sit in his ornate, self-decorated theater for hours at a time. He would watch news reels and original film footage of both Adolf Hitler and Benito Mussolini. It blended the reality of his life into what could have been, had he remained in Sicily.

"Get up, quick!" whispered Dom, as he shook Tony out of a very peaceful sleep.

"What for? Leave me alone," Tony mumbled.

"Come on! You'll like this," Dom insisted.

Tony sat up in bed and stared at Dom in total confusion.

"What are you talking about?" asked Tony. "What time is it?"

"One in the morning—we're going to the movies."

"The movies! Now I'm convinced that you have truly lost what was left of your mind," Tony said as he crawled back into his warm bed.

"Just shut up and follow me!" said Dom as he pulled him up and jerked him through the doorway.

They went down the long dark hallway, then continued down the stairs to the main floor of the house and into the basement. Into the sanctuary of Joseph Julianno. They quietly slipped into the projection booth. Tony gazed with amazement through the porthole of glass. An original film clip of Mussolini giving a speech to a crowd of hundreds of thousands was playing on the screen.

"What are—"

Dominick quickly clamped his hand across Tony's mouth.

"Shhhh, he can't know we're here," whispered Dominick.

"What is he doing?" Tony asked, barely audible.

The bright spotlight was on Joseph Julianno, standing next to the screen. It was then that Tony realized that Mr. Julianno was wearing the exact same military outfit on Mussolini. He was lip-sinking Mussolini's speech. He was also mimicking each and every gesture being made by the Italian dictator.

"He's perfect!" Tony barely whispered. His eyes were glued to the figure as it moved in perfect synchronization to the character. It was at that time that Tony noticed that the height, width and angle of the screen made it appear as if Mr. Julianno was part of the film.

"He's even dressed like the guy!" Tony whispered to Dom.

"I know. He does this all the time," Dominick responded without taking his eyes off of his father. "He's watched so many of these films hundreds of times and has the dialogue and movements down perfectly. It's weird. He does everything Mussolini does when he does it. He raises his hand when he does. He pounds his fist when he does. It's like watching a 3D movie!"

"But why?" asked Tony.

"I'm not sure," said Dom. "It's something about wondering how he did it. How could he actually fool so many people for so long? I know he hates Mussolini, so I really don't understand."

They stayed in the projection room until the film was over. They then quickly and quietly hurried back to their beds. Tony laid awake the rest of the night with that bizarre scene playing over and over again in his mind.

The next day was Sunday, the first day of December. It was bright and cold and filled with mixed emotions for Tony as he attended a joyous and jubilant mass with the Julianno family. Joseph and Maria Julianno took great pride in showing off their soon-to-be priest son and his friend from the seminary. Except they now referred to Tony as their other son.

Dominick and Tony could not help but bask in the warmth of this newfound attention, perceived as symbols of holiness and innocence. Unfortunately, there was also a cloud of sadness hanging over that glorious December morning. This was the last day of their holiday and they were to report back to the Academy by six o'clock to resume their school schedule the following morning.

That afternoon, after mass and an enormous lunch, Tony, Dom and Joseph Julianno took a walk in the huge gardens behind the Julianno home.

"I can't begin to thank you enough for the absolutely wonderful time I've had here," Tony said to Mr. Julianno.

"Oh, Tony!" Joseph spoke with absolute sincerity. "Maria and I truly do think of you as our other son. We love you very much."

Tony could see a small tear coming from Joseph's eye.

"You honor us with your precious friendship to our son. We want you to come again and again. Even after you are a priest, our home will always be your home." He then embraced Tony. As he wrapped his arms around Tony, the sweet scent of cherry tobacco filled Tony's nostrils.

"I thank God every day that Dom has a friend like you at the seminary," he continued. "I'm sure that you will also be a fine priest someday. Just like Dominick." Mr. Julianno stroked Tony's hair and smiled at him.

"Hey, what about me?" asked Dominick. "Can I also come back?"

"I don't know," laughed Joseph. "It depends on your attitude."

Their laughter seemed to bring new life to the otherwise cold and lifeless winter garden. The wind was cold and seemed to periodically penetrate their warm coats and heartfelt joy.

As Tony walked along the garden's cobblestone path, he couldn't help but look at Joseph Julianno with inquisitive eyes. He was a strikingly handsome man, who appeared to be well cared for. His tall stature, salt and pepper hair, and deep brown eyes only added to his distinction. His olive complexion and exaggerated body movements attested to his Italian heritage.

Joseph Julianno was also a very proud man.

"My family immigrated to this country some thirty-seven years ago from Palermo," said Joseph as he walked beside the two seminarians.

"I was only ten when we got here," he continued. "I'll never forget the night we left."

Joseph stopped and turned towards the boys. His stare was hollow and empty.

"Have I ever told you this story before?" he asked both Tony and Dominick.

They both slowly shook their heads.

"You told us how poor you were when you got here, many times over," said Dominick.

"But I don't think you ever told us why you left Italy," Tony answered.

"Sicily!" snapped Joseph. His tone momentarily startled Tony.

"I'm sorry I scared you," he said as he looked at Tony. He then made a grand gesture to the skies. "We are Sicilians, not Italians! It was the Italians who forced us to leave," he continued.

He then motioned for the boys to sit on a nearby bench. Joseph slowly shook his head as he sat next to them.

"Your great uncle John came to our villa that evening to warn us," he said. "He told us that the fascist dictator Benito Mussolini had ordered the arrest of all suspected Mafia members."

Tony suddenly turned towards Joseph Julianno. He had a million questions. This began to sound a lot like Bishop Paul's story about Adolph Hitler and the warning made by Dietrich Bonhoeffer.

"John told my father, Giuseppe, your grandfather, that arrangements had been made for us to leave for America that night. Your great grandfather, Giovanni, had made the arrangements for us to go by boat. Mussolini hated our family since we were people of great wealth and influence. He seized our money and our assets and was preparing to seize us."

Joseph grimaced as he continued. "We left our beloved Sicily that night with only the clothes on our backs. Mussolini's thugs later arrested your great grandfather. We never heard from him again. It is believed that he was tortured and killed by those Fascist bastards!" Joseph's face tightened with anger and then suddenly reddened with embarrassment.

It was the first time that Tony had seen him angry. He looked different. He appeared to darken.

"I am so very sorry!" Joseph spoke in a flustered and mortified tone. "I did not intend to use such a word in the presence of two very holy children of the church."

"That's okay," said Tony as he nodded in understanding. "I'm sure we'll hear a lot worse in the confessional."

Joseph smiled and reached out to stroke Tony's hair.

"I'm sure you will, my sons," he answered.

"But Daddy, how do you know that it was the police who did that to Papa Giovanni?"

A puzzled look played across Joseph Julianno's face. "What do you mean?"

"I saw the pictures," answered Dominick. "I accidentally found them in your desk drawer."

"You mean the pictures of Papa's body?" Joseph appeared to be slightly surprised.

Dominick only nodded.

"Friends of our family," Joseph turned towards Tony as he spoke, "sent us the pictures after they found Papa's… that's what I called him—" Joseph's voice began to crack.

Dominick quickly moved over and embraced his father.

Joseph pulled his son even closer. He then reached over and pulled Tony close too. Tony was touched.

"They were pictures of my grandfather's mutilated body." A tear came to Joseph Julianno's eye. "I'm so sorry that you had to see them," he said as he kissed the top of Dominick's head. "I loved Papa very much, and I would never wish for you to see him butchered like that."

"I know the police killed him," said Joseph as he straightened himself and looked down at Dominick. "Their whole purpose was to destroy the Mafia, and they thought they could do it by killing off the heads of each family. Mussolini believed if he killed the *capo* the body would die."

Joseph stood and looked at the boys.

"Benito Mussolini," continued Joseph, "was a disgusting and greedy fool. He died a despicable and deserved death. But a thousand animals like Mussolini were not worth one Papa. I could never imagine how evil a person had to be to do that to an old man. I told myself that I would learn as much as I could about those animals. At first, I studied everything I could about them, just to get revenge. Now they are both gone, but I'm never too old for revenge. I know a great deal about Benito Mussolini, his demented idol Adolf Hitler, and the people who followed them."

Now Tony knew the reason for the theater.

Joseph looked pale and drawn as he motioned for the future priests to start back towards the house.

As the three walked along the cold stone path that encircled the garden, Joseph Julianno put his arms around the two boys. Then the consigliore to the most powerful organized crime family in the country admitted that he once had desires of becoming a priest.

"What!" said Dom in total disbelief. "You've got to be kidding!"

"No," was Joseph's surprised answer. "Don't you think I'm good enough to be a priest?"

"What about me?" asked Dominick. "Where would I be if you had become a priest?"

A smile brightened Joseph Julianno's face; he pulled the two boys closer and continued to walk.

"So I guess you're glad I changed my mind," he laughed.

Dominick nodded in agreement as they approached the house.

"Is that what happened?" asked Tony. "You changed your mind?"

As Joseph stepped forward to open the back door, he suddenly stopped and turned to face the boys.

"No," he said looking at Tony admiringly. "You are a very perceptive young man."

Tony looked down and smiled sheepishly.

"I'm serious," said Joseph, as he gently lifted Tony's chin with his left hand. "You seem to be able to tell if people are being completely honest or not."

Joseph bent slightly so that he could look directly into Tony's eyes.

"It's the eyes, isn't it?" stated Joseph. "You can tell by looking at a person's eyes, can't you?"

Tony's nod was involuntary, his face taking on a chalky appearance.

"There's no need to be afraid, my son," smiled Joseph, as the color began to return to Tony's cheeks. "You have a gift! You have a God-given gift! Somehow, you could tell that I wasn't being completely honest about changing my mind," said Joseph, as he gently removed his hand from supporting Tony's chin. "It was my father's idea, not mine, that I would become a lawyer."

Joseph then straightened and opened the door.

"Someday, when we have more time together," smiled Joseph, "I'll tell you the whole story. For now, however, I'm sure that Dominick agrees with my father that the priesthood is not my calling."

Dominick smiled and vigorously nodded in agreement.

It was at that moment that Tony did look deeply into Joseph Julianno's eyes. He truly did have a gift, and he truly did understand who this consigliore really was.

EIGHTEEN

With the Thanksgiving holidays ended, school slowly gained some sense of normalcy. It was on that Tuesday afternoon that Sean Walsh, the newly appointed dean, made an announcement during lunch that there would be a mandatory meeting for all seminarians in the school chapel, immediately after the meal was completed.

"Do not go back to your rooms or your classes," Sean emphasized. "Go straight to the chapel."

"Do I need to do or prepare anything?" Tony asked Sean.

"No," Sean said. "It's not going to be a religious service of any kind. It's just an important information meeting."

Tony nodded.

Immediately after lunch the entire school, including the faculty, gathered in the school chapel. The message was given twice by Sean Walsh. It was his first official announcement and he wanted to be sure that it was correctly heard by everyone.

"I guess you know what that's about," said Dominick, looking at Tony.

"Not really," shrugged Tony.

"Did you notice that Father Ferran wasn't there to greet us yesterday morning?" asked Dom.

"That was strange," Tony acknowledged. "I see what you're getting at!"

"They're going to make the announcement today," smiled Dom. "I'm sure of it."

"I really don't understand," said Robert. "What kind of announcement are you sure of?"

"I bet it's the new prior," said Greg Green as he waited on the table.

"I guess you're right." Tony made a half-hearted attempt at smiling; it would never be the same without his dear friend.

"So do you think that they'll tell us who the new prior will be?" asked Robert.

"No," answered Dominick. "They'll probably want us to guess until we get it right."

"Cut it out, Dom," said Tony. "He was asking a reasonable question."

Dominick just rolled his eyes.

"I'm sure that if it's about the new prior," Tony answered, "they'll tell us who it is. I would be surprised if he wasn't already here."

Tony then noticed Dominick glance towards the head table.

"You don't think it'll be Father Ferran, do you?" Tony asked in surprise.

Dominick shook his head.

"Why not? He's the principal and obviously next in line."

"It won't be him." Dominick seemed very sure of himself.

Tony's look went from curiosity to inquisitiveness. He noticed that it was making Dominick uncomfortable.

"You know who it is, don't you?" said Tony. "It's written all over your face, and the rest of your body is saying that you're hiding something."

"All right! All right!" Dominick whispered, as he threw up his arms. "I swear, you'd make a great police interrogator. You might have the wrong calling."

"No." Tony smiled. "I just know you."

Dominick slid his chair closer to Tony's. He then leaned over, as if he was about to divulge top secret information.

"You know that my father has connections." Dominick's voice was barely audible.

"Yeah," said Tony, straining to hear. "He should because of what he does, but what do they have to do with us?"

"It's not just that kind of connections. He knows a lot of really important people."

"Like who?"

"Quit interrupting!" Dominick admonished. "Do you want to hear this or not?"

"Sorry," smiled Tony, giving Dom his complete attention.

"That's better," said Dominick. "Because of all the money he gives to the church, he and the cardinal, the one and only Francis Joseph Spellman—you know, the one that was here at Bishop Paul's retirement—well, they are close friends."

"Really?" Tony's eyes widened.

Dominick nodded, raising his hand to remind Tony to quit interrupting. Tony nodded in acknowledgment.

"While we were home over the holidays," Dominick continued in his clandestine manner, "my father heard a rumor that the cardinal was recommending to the Order of Saint Augustine and the Governing Board of Augustinian Academy that a friend of Bishop Paul's be made prior."

Dominick then looked at Tony in a soulful way. "I would have said something to you, but I wasn't sure if you knew the guy or not."

"Do you know his name?" Tony asked.

"It's some priest named Coffer. I think it's John Coffer."

Tony looked puzzled.

"Did the Monsignor, I mean Bishop, ever mention this guy?" Dominick asked.

Tony shook his head. "I never heard of him."

"Oh well," Dominick shrugged. "I guess we'll find out after lunch."

"I guess so," Tony agreed. "Was that all he said about the guy, that he was a friend of Bishop Peter Paul's?"

"The only thing he added was that Coffer was a tight-fisted administrator from a large church in Boston. He described him as a tried and tested bureaucrat of the highest order. A real politician."

"Oh, great!" Tony said, shaking his head. "That's all we need around here is some politician."

NINETEEN

As the seminarians gathered in the chapel on that Saturday of August 29, 1959, it brought back memories of Tony's first arrival to "the hill." As Tony looked at the unchanging, drab green walls and checkered linoleum floor of the hallway that led to the chapel, he felt a sense of nostalgia. He also felt sad and apprehensive. This puzzled him.

"Look at 'em," said Dominick, as he nodded towards the freshmen. "They're like scared rabbits."

"I know," said Tony as he turned into the main entrance of the chapel. "We were the same when we were freshmen."

When he and Dominick arrived at the set of pews marked off for juniors, they genuflected at the same time. They then slipped into the pews, sat, and waited.

It had always been a tradition for the seniors to walk in with the faculty and staff. It was also considered fashionable for them to come in a few minutes late. That was why the lonely figure seated in the center of the row of chairs lined up in front of the altar seemed very out of place. A chill went up Tony's spine as he studied the man who occupied that central seat. He appeared to be in his mid-forties and highly distinguished. He had a commanding presence and impeccable posture.

"I bet that's him," whispered Dominick as he nudged Tony in the side.

Tony only nodded slightly as his eyes were transfixed upon this person.

Father Ferran's steps seemed to quicken when he caught sight of the stranger already seated. The other members of the faculty also picked up their pace as they followed Father Ferran. A sudden hush came over the seniors as they quickly slid into their assigned pews. The stranger seemed to be looking at his watch as he glared at Father Ferran coming down the aisle. Father Ferran, and his entourage, made a half-hearted attempt at genuflecting as they quickly went to their assigned seats.

"I guess they're more concerned about his feelings than God's," Tony whispered to Dom.

The stranger held out his right hand as if he expected it to be kissed as Father Ferran sat beside him. They exchanged a few whispered words, and Father Ferran quickly went to the podium and adjusted the microphone.

"Are we all here?" he asked, nervously, as he looked in the direction of the newly appointed Dean of Postulants.

Sean Walsh only nodded in his direction.

"Good!" said Father Ferran as he cleared his throat. "I ... I mean, *we*," gesturing towards the entire faculty, "have a very special announcement to make this afternoon."

Father John Ferran generally was a very calm person who would speak with both his mouth and his hands. Ordinarily his words were completely synchronized with his hand gestures. It was a special gift which he used very wisely. His speech was also very clear and his articulation was perfect.

All of the staff and faculty, now seated to the right and left of the stranger, simultaneously nodded, as if giving their approval to Father Ferran's statement. The stranger's face remained emotionless. That's why it seemed so strange to both Tony and Dominick. Father Ferran seemed confused and nervous. He used the wrong words and had to correct himself, which he had never done before.

"Why is he so nervous?" asked Dominick.

"It must be him," Tony said, secretly pointing towards the stranger next to Father Ferran.

Dominick nodded.

"As most of you know, I'm Father John Ferran, the school principal."

He rambled on for nearly ten minutes before he finally introduced the stranger as Monsignor John K. Coffer, the new school prior. He then groveled for another ten minutes as he explained how the now Bishop Paul had retired to Ettal and how Monsignor Coffer was handpicked by Cardinal Spellman himself.

Dominick nudged Tony again. Tony smiled and nodded again. Everything that Dominick had told him had proven to be correct. Dominick's father was very well informed, even to the point that Monsignor Paul's replacement was handpicked by Cardinal Francis Spellman.

"Gentlemen, I am honored and privileged to present to you our new leader, Reverend Monsignor John Coffer!"

Father Ferran began a loud and boisterous round of applause, which incited everyone to rise to their feet with a standing ovation. Even Tony was caught up in the act.

Their new leader coldly smiled as he ambled towards the podium. This time, however, he held out his right hand to the school principal and fully expected to have his ring kissed. John Ferran instinctively genuflected as he kissed the prior's ring. He then quickly stood, returning to his seat red-faced and embarrassed.

"Thank you, Father Ferran," he began.

It was immediately obvious that the new prior was no stranger to public speaking. His voice was deep and melodious. He could captivate an audience with nothing more than the tonal qualities of his voice. He truly was a politician.

Another thing that Joseph Julianno was correct about, Tony thought.

"I am both humbled and proud to be here. I also hope and pray that I can prove to be worthy of Cardinal Spellman's confidence in requesting that I take this distinguished position."

Father Ferran led off another round of pretentious applause, which he repeated on numerous occasions during the entirety of Monsignor Coffer's rather pompous proclamation. It was not until the last five minutes of his forty-five minute speech that the Monsignor finally broke away from self-acclaimed praises. He finally announced the official assignments and responsibilities for the upcoming year.

"All of you already know that Sean Walsh has been appointed as the dean of postulants. I personally wish to congratulate him on this achievement."

The applause for Sean was spontaneous and sincere.

"Richard O'Malley is appointed as assistant dean, and will serve as dean in the event that Dean Walsh is absent for any reason whatsoever. The individual who is appointed to be sacristan here at Augustinian Academy is Anthony Saleem."

Dominick immediately stood up and began a wild and tumultuous round of applause, which seemed to rival the applause given to the prior himself. This took the monsignor by surprise as he momentarily stepped back from the podium.

"I also want to make a very special announcement," he continued, as if to regain his composure. "We will be joined, in about a week, by two new staff members. Father Michael McCrane will be our new vice principal and head of discipline."

The announcement of a vice principal seemed to take Father Ferran by surprise.

"Sister Mary Ruth," continued the monsignor, "who is from Norway, will be joining our Daughters of the Holy Redeemer. She will serve as a member of our culinary and linen staff. Both of these individuals are brand new to Augustinian Academy, and Sister Mary Ruth is new to our country, so I expect that you will all make an extra effort to make them feel welcome and at home."

Father Ferran then asked the dean, assistant dean, and sacristan to wait after the assembly. He immediately dismissed the others.

As the seminarians began to file out of the chapel, Tony made his way to the front with Sean Walsh and Ritchie O'Malley. A tingling sense of pride mixed with excitement came over Tony as he felt the admiring eyes of his fellow postulants watching him.

"Our new prior wanted to personally meet you," explained Father Ferran, turning to begin the introductions.

"Monsignor, this is Sean Walsh, our new dean of postulants."

"Good afternoon, Sean," smiled the Monsignor, putting forth his right hand.

Sean instinctively grabbed it with both hands. He then genuflected as he kissed the signet ring on his third finger.

"You realize you don't have to do that," said the monsignor while he offered absolutely no resistance whatsoever.

"I think he's trying to show respect for your position," explained Father Ferran.

"I understand," acknowledged the monsignor, reveling in all of the attention.

As the prior gently raised Sean Walsh to his feet and looked directly into his eyes, Sean turned away in humility.

"You are a fine young man, Sean Walsh," the monsignor said softly. "Remember, I am only God's humble servant."

The pretentious charade continued with the introduction of Richard O'Malley as assistant dean. The pompous genuflecting, ring-kissing, and ass-kissing was a repeat of the Sean Walsh introduction.

"And this is Anthony Saleem," said Father Ferran, motioning towards Tony. "As you know, he's our new sacristan."

Tony only nodded and made no pretense of reaching for the monsignor's ring. The prior's hand suddenly stopped in mid-movement. He then slowly withdrew it to his side.

"I have a cold," explained Tony. "I really don't want to infect anyone else whose lips may come in contact with your ring."

It was obvious that the new head of Augustinian Academy didn't believe the newly appointed sacristan. It was equally obvious that the newly appointed sacristan didn't really care what his pompous new leader believed.

"I understand that you're only a junior," said the monsignor as he slid his right hand into the pocket of his red-fringed cassock. It was as if he were trying to protect it from the infectious germs of this insolent young seminarian.

"That's correct, Father."

"You mean Monsignor, don't you?" replied the prior.

"I'm sorry... I don't understand what you mean." Tony looked puzzled.

"You are to address me by my proper title," snapped Coffer. "And that title is MONSIGNOR!"

His raised voice echoed throughout the chapel; a deathly silence came over everyone who was present. As the prior saw the shocked look of each faculty member, he became flustered and embarrassed by his own outburst.

"I'm sorry," said Coffer, in a softer and more subdued voice. "I should not have snapped at you."

"That's okay, Father. I mean, Monsignor," nodded Tony.

The newly appointed prior bit his tongue.

"In answer to your original question," continued Tony, "I am only a junior. The position is traditionally filled by a member of the incoming junior class."

"What Tony is saying is correct," said Father Ferran. "It's a tradition which has been established for many years by our former priors.'

"Oh I'm sure it's correct," laughed Coffer. "I don't think that this junior seminarian would blatantly try to tell me a lie. You wouldn't! Would you?"

"Of course not, Monsignor. That would be a sin."

"Who decides on these positions?" Coffer asked Ferran.

"They're voted on by the faculty at the end of each school year," said Ferran. "Tony, however, was handpicked by the former prior, Bishop Peter J. Paul. He and Tony have been friends for many years."

"I understand," said the Prior. "How long have you known Bishop Paul?" Coffer asked Tony.

"Almost all of my life. He was the senior pastor of my parish church in Jacksonville, Florida."

"That's a long time," said Coffer. "Has he ever talked to you about Ettal?"

The question startled Tony. Why would he suddenly ask such a question?

"I'm not sure I heard you correctly," Tony said.

"It's not important," said the prior. "I was just making small talk, and I'm sure that each of you has to be getting back to class. We'll have plenty of time to talk later. I plan on being here a long time." He then smiled and graciously dismissed them.

He then turned towards Father Ferran. "I would like to further discuss these appointments with you, in private. I also want to discuss the assistant principle appointment with you, as well."

The newly appointed prior then turned towards the back of the sanctuary, as the dean, assistant dean, and sacristan filed out of their pews to leave. As Tony stepped into the center of the chapel aisle, in order to genuflect, he was directly in front of Monsignor Coffer. Tony slightly moved to his left to complete his genuflection. He could feel the Monsignor's eyes burning into him.

"Why did you move over?" asked Coffer.

"Just a habit," said Tony. "I don't like anything between me and God."

"I see," smiled Coffer. "Even Monsignors?"

Tony pretended not to hear as he turned and quickly walked from the chapel.

I can't believe I did that! thought Tony. *I probably screwed myself out of the dean's position for next year. There's no telling what else I ruined for myself. All because of my big mouth!*

"Why didn't I just kiss his ring," Tony said aloud, "or his ass?"

"What?" asked Dominick, startling Tony. "Kiss whose ass?"

"I'll explain it later. I'm just glad to see you. I really need a friend right now."

TWENTY

Out of all of his scheduled activities, it was the *magnum silentium* that seemed to bring the most anxiety to Tony. Thoughts of the "great silence" were accompanied with feelings of depression and a strong sense of alarm. The reasons for such feelings were far beyond his comprehension.

As Tony walked to his room from setting up in the chapel for the next morning's mass and services, he thought about his encounter with the new prior. He felt a strong chill come over his entire body.

The sharp sound of the bell interrupted his thoughts. It was time for lights out. With a faint smile, Tony went into his room, knowing that he was immune from having to do this. It was one of the many perks of the position of sacristan. Tony grabbed his leather bag of toiletries and opened the door to head to the lavatory area. He was suddenly startled by the appearance of the new prior in his doorway.

Tony's eyes widened as he stepped backwards. "I'm sorry..."

"No need to be sorry," said the prior. "I saw the light coming from under your door and I was wondering why it was still on? I thought it was the rules that all of the lights in the seminarians' rooms had to be turned out, and that each seminarian had to be in his bed, when the ten o'clock bell rang?"

"That's correct," said Tony, with a puzzled look. "I'm the sacristan and, since I usually work late setting up the chapel, I'm given an extra hour."

"Whose idea was that?" asked the monsignor.

"I honestly don't know," answered Tony. "It was one of the guidelines in The Seminarian's Handbook."

"Okay," said Coffer. "I'll check into it. In the meantime, get to bed as soon as you can. We have a full day tomorrow and you'll need your rest."

Tony smiled and continued towards the lavatory. Coffer reached into Tony's room and turned off the light.

When Tony returned to his room, he flipped the light back on. Not because he needed to, but because he wanted to. He then waited for a few minutes and flipped it off, jumped into bed, and hoped that sleep would come soon.

He thought of the happy and joyful conversation that he and Dom had in the courtyard earlier. His thoughts, however, slowly began to turn towards what his mother told him about his illness. A sense of numbness began to envelop his body. This sense of numbness and anxiety seemed to be magnified by the darkness which surrounded him.

Was he simply afraid of the dark or was it something far more significant? His thoughts made only cursory impressions on his brain.

As thoughts of his family began to flood into his mind, his fear and apprehension became more intense. He was becoming uncomfortable again. At that moment, however, a stranger and more unique feeling began to creep into his conscience. The anxiety he felt was mixed with a deep sense of curiosity.

Why don't I want to think about them? he thought. *Why do I feel so empty? And why am I beginning to feel so scared?*

Tony slowly, but cautiously, gave in to the pull of his emotions. He let his mind reflect on his brother Johnny and his sister Cecelia. His apprehension began to further give way to his curious desires. He allowed himself the strange pleasure of thinking about the things that caused him so much fear. The knowledge that they were so far away did cause him to feel sad and lonely. The fear and apprehension he once felt slowly began to subside. He was soon wondering why he ever worried about it in the first place. It wasn't until he was at the very edge of sleep that he became overwhelmed with depression.

He then began to think about his older brother Fred Jr., the one that everybody called Freddie Boy. Fred hated that nickname. He had joined the Army again last year and, within a month, he had been discharged. Tony tried to picture his brother carrying a rifle and marching through the woods. Suddenly he was overcome with a strange fear.

Tony couldn't understand why he didn't feel the same way about Freddie Boy as he did about Cecelia and Johnny.

"I love Johnny and Cecelia," he thought. "I really don't love Freddy Boy. I'm not sure what I feel for him." Tony heard himself speaking out loud. He quickly stopped for fear that someone might hear him.

Tony also couldn't understand why he loved to think of his brother as Freddie Boy. He equally loved the thought that the name caused his brother so much pain. It would throw Freddie Boy into a rage. There was something else that threw him into an even greater fury.

I just can't remember what it is! Tony thought. *It's like it was erased from my memory.*

A sudden pain shot through Tony's head, as if a lightning bolt had hit him.

"I had better stop this," Tony said. "Things are happening that I truly don't understand." Beads of sweat formed on Tony's forehead. His eyes suddenly popped open. He felt pain, real pain, in the back of his head. "Why do I hate him?"

Tony sat up in his metal framed bed, which looked more like a cot than a bed. He could feel the sweat as it rolled down his sides and the right side of his head. He was also cold. The mixture of sweat and cold scared the young seminarian.

He absolutely did not understand his feelings. He knew he should love his brother. He knew that most people would fight with their siblings; but in spite of everything else, they shared a family love for one another. He truly did hate his older brother. He felt nothing but contempt.

What did he do to me? he thought. *How could he have hurt me? Surely I would remember something like that.* His thoughts were painful, but blurred. He laid his head back on his slightly damp pillow.

"I don't want to think about him anymore," Tony said aloud. He deliberately directed his thought to other things.

He let his mind dwell on his mother's face. He thought about how much older she looked when he saw her at the bus station the past summer. He asked God to help him go to sleep. God answered his prayer. He physically went to sleep, but, for some unclear reason, God let him dream.

"I guess you don't notice a person aging when you see them every day," Tony said at the beginning of his dream.

As the dream continued Tony thought about the strange thing his mother said about her white hair. It was even stranger the way she described his illness. She acted as if it were normal for him to have all three of these diseases at the same time. If that were true, he should have been in Ripley's *Believe it or Not*.

His troubled sleep began to engulf him. Sporadic flashes filled his brain. He drifted back to a time when he was only six or seven years old. He could still see his mother's face looming over his bed. Her face was covered with tears, but it was hard and guilt-ridden. It was the time when he was ill. He was deathly ill. Suddenly another face appeared, on the other side of the bed.

"Dr. Temples!" Tony's words were almost audible as he was pulled deeper into his sleep.

"I don't think he'll make it through the night!" The doctor's words were crisp and clear. "We need to get him to a hospital."

The expression on his mother's face changed to raw fear.

"Laht!" His father's voice seemed to fill the room. It was the same tone which he used to stop his mother on Christmas Day. It was the "laht" of "Stop it and get a grip!"

"I don't understand," Dr. Temples said.

Tony seemed to understand the Lebanese word. After all it was a dream.

"No!" repeated his father in English. "We won't take him to the hospital. We'll take better care of him here."

The doctor's face and the entire room seemed to be in a fog and everything was blurry. The only thing that was clear now was his mother's face. He could see the tears running down her cheeks. He remembered looking deeply into her eyes. He searched for the truth.

The truth about what? His mind was racing.

Her face seemed to be caught somewhere between guilt and terror. He saw her eyes. Then a bright light seemed to flash. The roomed darkened. A cold sweat came over Tony's entire body. His mother's face was clearly outlined, especially her hair. It was as white as snow.

As the young seminarian lay on his bed on that cold winter night, he could feel sweat on the back of his neck. An overwhelming sense of fear continued to sweep over him. He desperately tried to look deeper into her eyes, but he just couldn't pull his eyes away from her hair. The absolute whiteness of her hair burned its way into his mind. It looked like the hair of a corpse!

He suddenly bolted from his sleep. His body once more was covered in sweat.

"What the hell happened?" His thoughts were clouded. He felt disoriented. His hands tightly clinched the covers and his knuckles turned white. Hearing the sounds of his own voice woke him.

"It was a dream," he said. "It was only a dream."

He had created his own dream by lulling himself to sleep with thoughts of his family. It was only a dream.

But it was real, he thought as he sat up in bed. *The things I thought were real! They actually did happen. How could I have been sleeping?*

Tony's eyes caught a glimpse of the clock on the chest of drawers.

Three-thirty! he thought. *I guess I did fall asleep. I guess it must have been a dream.*

He could still feel the cold sweat on his body. His mind felt like it was submerged in a sea of emotions. Sensations of fear, anxiety, and guilt rushed through him and splashed against his very soul. As the future priest sat in his bed in his cell-like room in Augustinian Academy, he began to tremble. It was as if he was locked in a shivering trance. It was as if the very essence of his being was trapped between his burning desire to know the truth and the absolute fear of discovering it.

Tony knew that there was more to this dream. More than he would want to know. His feelings were real, but masked. Why did he hate his older brother so much? Why couldn't he see love in his mother's eyes? Especially when she thought he was dying? Why was there so much fear and guilt on her face? Why was he so afraid? Why did her hair remind him of death?

134

Why was I so afraid? he thought. *Was it death? Was I afraid of dying? Did I even know what death meant?*

As he tried desperately to push the thoughts of his mother's face from his mind, he caught one last glimpse of those tear-filled eyes and the ghost-like appearance of that white hair. What deep hidden emotions did she blur with her tears? He truly hoped it was love, but he knew that it wasn't.

I've got to know, he thought, *but I'm afraid.*

It was at that moment that Tony knew that his burning curiosity would carry him to a place where he did not want to be. His inquisitive mind would be pushed and shoved through a doorway. A doorway that was so terrifying that the very core of his soul had bolted it shut. He began to tremble uncontrollably. He prayed again, but in a way that he never had prayed before. He literally talked to God as a child would speak to a loving father. He told Him how scared he was and how much he needed the rest. It was as if his Loving Father gently laid Tony's damp head back on his suddenly dry pillow. Tony's mind went blank. He was overcome by a deep restful sleep.

TWENTY-ONE

Tony had a basic philosophy about life. He simply felt that the simplest solution was usually the best. He used this philosophy in his dealings with Monsignor John Coffer. He wanted to just do what the man asked and stay out of his way. The sacristan felt extremely uncomfortable when the prior was around. He not only made him feel uncomfortable, but the Prior was also very demeaning. Coffer's criticism of Tony's work was not in any way constructive. It aimed for humiliation.

The newly appointed sacristan's duties and responsibilities were outlined in a handbook, *The Daily Activities and Holy Responsibilities of the Sacristan*. This was Tony's bible, and he followed it to the letter. Tony realized very early in his seminary career that he was blessed with a photographic memory. It always surprised him when his fellow students and postulant brothers had difficulty memorizing phrases and definitions. All he had to do was read them from the imprint on his mind. Dominick was the first to point out to him that this was an extraordinary gift not possessed by everyone. Tony had memorized the sacristan's handbook, and he was very knowledgeable of his duties and responsibilities. He also took them very seriously.

It was the basic responsibility of the sacristan to prepare the chalice and to lay out the priest's vestments before mass. First he would set up the chalice with its appurtenances. The chalice itself was a cup that was made of gold or silver. The interior of the chalice was always lined with pure gold. Its purpose was to hold the wine for the Holy

Sacrifice. The Holy Sacrifice was the ritual held by all Catholics, in which the priest, according to Catholic doctrine, miraculously transformed the wine in the chalice into the true blood of Jesus Christ. It was for this basic reason that great care had to be taken in setting up this very sacred vessel.

Once the chalice was perfect, Tony would then tackle the vestments.

The vestments are all laid out in reverse order, as to how they are worn by the priest celebrating the mass. This is done in order to easily accommodate the priest. The first item laid out was the one put on last. This is the chasuble. The stole is then placed across the top and along the sides of the chasuble. The maniple is then placed on top of the left side of the stole. Then the cincture. The alb is next. The alb is a white linen robe covering the entire body of the priest. It is significant in that the priest sometimes turns the vesting prayer of the alb into a blessing. This is a very private blessing, however, that generally a priest says to himself.

The vesting prayer for the alb is simply: "Make me white, O Lord, and cleanse my heart; that being made white in the blood of the lamb I may deserve an eternal reward." The entire vesting prayer is said in Latin. The blessing, however, is only whispered by the priest and spoken in any language he chooses. It is generally either the language of his native tongue or Latin. The blessing is simply the act of asking God to bless his actions and activities before others as he is an *alter Christos,* which means another Christ.

The final vestment that is put in place is the amice. This is an oblong piece of fine linen. The vesting priest places it for a moment on his head, and then allows it to rest upon his shoulders. He then ties it in place with two long white linen straps. The amice represents the helmet of salvation. In spite of the fact that it only briefly rests on the head, it still is representative of a protective helmet.

All of the vestments had to be laid out exactly as he described. There was no margin for error. The young seminarian understood the sacredness of the mass, but Coffer seemed to put a lot more emphasis on the ritual of the mass than he did on the meaning of the mass.

It was more important to Monsignor Coffer to have the stole that a priest wore while celebrating mass laid out to his specifications than it was to celebrate the Mass with a sense of reverence and humility. Coffer would constantly complain to the young sacristan that the vestments were incorrectly presented, as he would put it. A certain corner of a vestment was not at just the right angle. The top and bottom cords of the amice had to crossover at the exact same distance. The back of the chasuble had to be folded perfectly. This would "allow it to be presented perfectly," as the narcissistic monsignor would say.

He flips the damned thing on, thought Tony. *Who in the world is he wanting to see him make a perfect presentation? There's no one here but he and I. I'm the only audience he has. And I'm damned sure not the one he's trying to impress!* Tony struck the top of the vestibule with his fist. The small silver plate, which ordinarily held the eucharist, went flying to the other side of the room.

Tony quickly went to retrieve it. It was at that moment that he first saw it. It appeared to be a small button glued to the wall. It was barely visible. In fact, it almost perfectly blended in with the dark paneling of the room. It was about eighteen inches from the floor, and you had to be almost on top of it and looking directly at it in order to see it.

What is it? thought Tony as he touched it with the tips of his fingers.

As he pulled back on it, it gave way. A plug, which was exactly two inches square, pulled out of the wall.

"I don't give a damn what they want!" snapped Coffer.

Tony jumped back from the wall.

"My God!" the sacristan mumbled. "It leads to the prior's room!"

As Tony leaned forward to replace the plug, he could distinctly hear the prior vehemently yelling at someone or something.

There's no telling how long it's been there, thought Tony. *Either some past sacristan or even a priest must have set it up in order to eavesdrop on the prior. Why would they want to do that?*

It was only a matter of time before Tony would truly realize the importance of this discovery.

TWENTY-TWO

Early one morning of November 1959, a simple disagreement between Tony and the prior came to an explosive head. Prior Coffer declared that the sacristan should kneel and kiss his alb prior to his adorning it.

Tony disagreed.

"The blessing of the alb is a very holy time," said Coffer. "It is not to be taken lightly."

"It is also a private prayer," interrupted Tony. "The sacristan's handbook describes it as a time that is to be shared between the vesting priest and God, and no one else."

"All the more reason for you to participate by kneeling and kissing the damn..." Coffer stopped mid-word. "I mean, kissing the alb."

"Then that would mean that I would have to disregard the orders of the sacristan's handbook," retorted Tony. "It even says that it would be best for the sacristan to completely leave the vestibule during the blessing of the alb."

"I really don't care what that stupid book says," Coffer snapped back. "When I say kneel, I want you to kneel!"

That evening, during the magnum silentium, Coffer apologized to the young sacristan.

"I really shouldn't have gotten so upset with you this morning," the Monsignor said in a very soft and subdued voice.

Tony only nodded since only an ordained priest could speak during the "great silence."

"Go ahead! You can speak," said Coffer as if he were giving him a special dispensation.

Tony only shook his head, displaying his reverence and strict adherence of the rules of the Academy.

Coffer's face turned bright red. Tony looked directly into his eyes. Tony looked past the anger, which burned through the prior, and could see the inexplicable emotion of fear.

He's afraid of something. What could it be?

His answer came from the monsignor's own mouth.

"I shouldn't have told you that the sacristan's handbook was a stupid book." Coffer cleared his throat. "It is probably the most brilliantly written and most correct book of our century."

The author's name flashed through Tony's photographic memory. He smiled

Of course!. It was Cardinal Spellman's book. It was written by then Monsignor Francis J. Spellman.

TWENTY-THREE

"He never kneels when I'm giving my blessing to the alb," said Coffer to Father Michael McCrane, the newly appointed vice principal and disciplinarian.

"I don't understand," replied McCrane in a puzzled tone.

Coffer sternly looked at McCrane as they sat across from each other in huge armchairs decorating the monsignor's newly renovated living chambers. They sipped white wine.

"He's irreverent!" snapped Coffer, startling McCrane, who almost spilled his wine.

"He obviously upsets you," replied McCrane, trying to regain his composure. "So, why don't you just get rid of him?"

"How am I supposed to do that?" Coffer's face began to redden. "Maybe I should offer him up as a *human sacrifice*, instead of the Eucharist during mass."

"You could just expel him," replied the vice principal, trying to soften Coffer's mood.

"We can't just expel him," mimicked Coffer. "Priests are rare these days, according to the Vatican. We have to have a proper and acceptable reason. They call it just cause. And besides, he's got that damned prior's scholarship. The one that Peter Paul gave him!"

"Well!" said McCrane. "I guess you do need just cause. But I still don't get it. What is it about this kid that pisses you off so much? And don't give me that blessing of the alb crap!"

"You're right," snipped Coffer. "You're an asshole, but you're right."

Coffer took another sip of his wine and leaned back in his overstuffed chair.

"That's a good way of describing him," smiled Coffer. "He really does piss me off. It's his arrogant attitude." Coffer looked off into the distance.

"He questions everything," continued Coffer. "It's not only the simple things like laying out vestments before mass, but the very basics of everything I want him to do. He has little or no respect for me. He even acts like he's not afraid of me. He acts like he has something on me. Even worse, he might even know something about me."

A slight smile played across Michael McCrane's lips as he looked at Coffer.

"You don't believe me! Do you?" The monsignor looked irritated, his eyes locking on to McCrane's.

"If you say it, I believe it." McCrane shrugged his shoulders.

"That's exactly what I mean," Coffer said as he adjusted himself in his chair. "This Saleem kid doesn't know me as well as you do, but he is just as arrogant as you!"

McCrane stiffened at the remark.

"Don't get your shorts in a wad," snarled Coffer. "What I'm really trying to say is this kid could be dangerous."

"Dangerous!" laughed McCrane, with an incredulous look. "You've got to be kidding. He's a sixteen-year old postulant who doesn't know his ass from a cincture!"

The monsignor surprisingly smiled as he shook his head and looked down.

"You mean his sphincter from a cincture."

McCrane stopped in mid-sip. He then burst into hysterical laughter. Blowing and spilling wine all over himself and the brand new, beautifully upholstered chair in which he sat. Coffer momentarily froze in anger, his beautiful chair being irreparably stained by his vice principal. His stiffened facial muscles began to relax, however, as he realized that McCrane really was enjoying his joke.

"That... That's..." gasped McCrane. "That's the funniest..."

"Just calm down, Father McCrane," smiled Coffer. "Take a deep breath and speak slowly."

"That's the funniest joke I've ever heard you tell," said McCrane, still gasping.

Coffer continued to smile as he leaned forward and touched his head disciplinarian's shoulder.

"In fact," continued McCrane. "I think it's the only time I've ever heard you tell a joke."

"I probably should try to be a little more humorous. It is more relaxing, and I'd probably live a lot longer without all this stress."

"You're damned right you would!'

"I am serious about this Anthony Saleem," continued the monsignor. "He really could be dangerous, and I'm not sure how much he knows."

"What do you mean?" McCrane asked. He vainly attempted to wipe the wine stains from the chair with his handkerchief.

"He makes some strong arguments against the rituals and traditions of our faith. The little bastard sometimes even causes me to question a few things, privately, of course." Coffer looked down at the floor. "It makes me wonder if he knows more about Catholic doctrine than I do."

"Maybe you should have studied it more when you had the chance. You had to know that this whole masquerade would not be easy," McCrane said.

"Do not ever speak of that again!"

"It slipped out." McCrane looked at Coffer with disgust, then abruptly changed the subject. "What does the kid argue about?"

"Simple things, things we have accepted as clear and uncomplicated church doctrines. Like eating meat on Friday and the fact that it's a mortal sin."

"So, what's he questioning?" McCrane stopped wiping and looked up at Coffer.

"He asks crazy crap," replied Coffer, waving his arm above his head. "If someone eats meat on Friday and dies with a mortal sin on his soul, then does that means he goes to hell? I tell him yes, that person will go to hell for all eternity."

The monsignor's face begins to become flush.

"The son of a bitch then hits me with a real zinger," continues Coffer, becoming more irate. "He says that can't be correct. That would mean that one man is condemning another man to hell. God is the only one who can judge and condemn someone to eternal hell. Not man."

Father Michael McCrane dropped the handkerchief and stood. He had a puzzled look as he stared directly down at the monsignor.

"I don't understand," said the vice principal. "I'm not that drunk. What the hell does he mean by all that bullshit?"

"That bullshit, my friend," smiled the monsignor, "is exactly what I'm talking about. This kid is dangerous!"

Coffer takes a deep breath before he drives home his final point.

"A law is something made up by a human being, since it's not in the bible, which, if broken, causes another human being to be condemned to hell, makes that human being equal to God."

"How?" asked McCrane, his mouth gapping open.

The Monsignor spoke slowly and deliberately, as if he were shoving a knife into McCrane's questioning heart.

"It forces God to send a person to hell for something that He, as God, did not ordain!"

It only took a second for it to sink into Father Michael McCrane's brain as he stared in total shock at the monsignor.

"My God!" said the vice principal in a cracked voice. "How did you answer him?"

"I guess I lost it," said Coffer very coldly. "I asked him—without thinking, of course—why in the world was he reading and interpreting the Bible? He was nothing but an ignorant seminarian. Only an ordained priest could interpret the Bible. Private interpretation of the Bible was against the doctrine of the Holy Catholic Church!"

Monsignor Coffer then paused for effect.

"In fact," continued Coffer, "my answer was given to him in a rather vehement manner."

"I bet it was," said McCrane, slowly nodding. "Did he answer you?"

Coffer shook his head. "He only smiled."

"You're right," McCrane agreed with Coffer. "He's one smart kid. Still, I don't see how he could be dangerous. He's still a postulant and you're the prior. If he irritates you too much, just expel his ass! Don't give me that crap about the shortage of priests. You know what you really can do."

"You're right!" Coffer leaned back in the chair and placed his arms across his chest. "Sometimes you are very perceptive."

McCrane smiled.

"The most worst of all things," Coffer's words were slurred.

"I don't think that's good English," said McCrane, who was also drunk. "Or is it well English?"

"You asshole! Just listen to me for one minute!" Coffer's speech got worse. "That prick Saleem has known Peter Paul a long time. Hell, Peter Paul practically raised the kid. I truly don't know what he shared with the little bastard. I don't know what he told him."

"What the hell—" McCrane froze. "You don't honestly think that he said anything to him about Ettal, do you?"

"That's just it," the prior answered. "I don't know, but we absolutely have to find out! That's why we can't get rid of him until we do know for sure."

"I see your point." McCrane raised his glass to Coffer. "I'll take care of it, ole Buddy."

"Quit calling me 'ole Buddy,'" Coffer finally gave the semblance of a drunken smile. He then raised his glass to McCrane.

"I know you will. That's why I hard-pickled you for this job."

"No!" McCrane spilled his wine on Coffer's cassock.

"You drunken piece of shit!" Coffer yelled.

"I'm sorry." McCrane stood up and made a sad attempt of trying to wipe the mess with his already stained handkerchief. He stumbled and fell flat on his face, next to the fireplace. McCrane did not miss a beat. "You picked me because of Ettal."

"First of all," slurred Coffer. "I did nothing to Bonhoeffer! You're the one who actually hung him, you sadistic bastard! Then you filmed it, in order to kiss your Fuhrer's ass. That's why I picked you! You like to put your nose up your superior's asses. You actually like to suck up and kiss ass."

"You really are a bastard!" said McCrane, looking up at Coffer from the floor. "You are nothing but a coldblooded prick. Don't ever say that man's name around here again. Do you understand me?"

McCrane pushed himself up to a sitting position. He looked up at Coffer with his now blood red eyes. "You know what I'm capable of, don't you? I think you have a good idea as to what I'll do to you if you ever threaten me again. You're nothing but a..."

McCrane stood on his feet. He appeared to be completely sober, but enraged. "You disgusting worm," he continued as he lifted Coffer off his feet by his throat. "You're nothing but a *polizeispitzel!*" He then dropped Coffer on the floor. As Coffer was gasping for breath, he threw up.

"That's disgusting!" McCrane said. "Why don't you get your little prick Saleem in here to clean that shit up? I'm going to bed."

McCrane left Coffer lying in his own vomit, still gasping for air.

Tony gently replaced the square listening plug. He then backed away. Sweat covered his head and body. He was scared. Very, very scared. He too wanted to vomit.

Tears welling up in his eyes, Tony slowly walked out of the sanctuary and then out of the chapel—keeping a careful lookout, all the way to his room, for the Fuhrer-loving vice principal.

TWENTY-FOUR

"I thought your scholarship was for life or at least until you graduated from the Academy," said Robert.

"Monsignor Peter Paul told me that no one could ever take it away from me," answered Tony.

"I really don't think that our new prior gives a damn about the wishes of our former prior," Dominick said sarcastically.

"You really shouldn't curse," replied Robert.

"If you think that was cursing," said Tony, "I'm glad you didn't hear Monsignor Coffer and Father McCrane last night."

"I can't believe they said all that," said Dom, shaking his head. "Hell! They're supposed to be priests! You said that they were just outside the door when you heard them, and they were drunk?"

"Yes," Tony said reluctantly, not wanting to tell Dom the truth in front of Robert.

"Well that sucks," said Dom, "and those two are real bastards."

"There goes that filthy mouth of yours again," said Robert.

"Be quiet!" snapped Dom. "If you aren't going to do anything but complain, why don't you just get out of here?"

"It isn't going to do any good for us to fight," said Tony. "I really need your help. I'm scared, Dom! I'm really scared!"

Tony's face looked pale and drawn, and Dom studied him for a moment. He wanted to help his friend, but he just didn't know how. He was also scared. His instincts immediately took control, and his sense of humor kicked in.

"Don't worry, Tony," smiled Dom. "I'll call my dad, and he'll have a couple of wise guys visit the Monsignor and his new head disciplinarian. They'll simply put them to *sleep with the fishes*."

"What does that mean?" asked Robert. "I really don't know what that means. I didn't think fish ever slept."

Dominick looked directly at Robert. He leaned in slightly to study his face.

"You're serious, aren't you? You really don't know what that means."

"I really don't," said Robert, shaking his head.

Dominick burst into laughter, gently grabbing Robert by the shoulder.

"You really know when to bring in the comic relief, don't you?" Dominick pulled Robert closer to him.

Robert simply shrugged his shoulders and looked totally baffled.

Tony joined in the laughter, taking Robert's opposite shoulder.

"I don't know what we're going to do," laughed Tony as he looked directly at Robert, "when you finally do grow up."

Robert, not sure as to what was happening, reluctantly joined in the laughter. All he knew was that, somehow, he made his friends happy. To Robert, that was all that mattered.

Their joviality was suddenly interrupted by the distinct sound of Father McCrane's voice coming from behind them.

"Isn't it almost time for study, boys?"

As McCrane towered over the three young postulants sitting on the courtyard bench, they had to twist their necks and lift their head upwards to see his face. Robert was still smiling as he looked up at the six-foot five-inch disciplinarian.

The sudden snapping of McCrane's cincture against Robert's mouth made him jerk backwards and slam into Tony's right eye.

"Are you crazy?" Tony cried and covered his eye with his right hand.

McCrane's movements were deliberate and calculating as he grasped Tony's hand and pulled it away.

"I'll show you who's crazy," said McCrane.

He lashed the cincture against Tony's injured eye.

For a brief second and through a blur of pain, Tony looked into the eyes of his assailant. He looked beyond the blood red that spread to the edge of his pupils, to the very essence of McCrane's soul. He could only see evil, pure evil.

As a sinister smile began to form on the head disciplinarian's lips, he raised the leather cincture preparing to strike Tony again.

"What is going on?" someone yelled from across the courtyard.

McCrane stopped in mid-strike and released Tony's hand.

"Nothing, Father," said McCrane, in a monotone voice.

As Father Ferran approached, he looked at the faces of the three young seminarians. He attempted to hide his shocked expression, but he finally had to look away.

"What happened here?" he demanded.

"I was simply doing my job," said McCrane. His spoke in a sarcastic and patronizing tone.

"Horsewhipping children is not your job!" Ferran stated loudly.

"Isn't it unprofessional, unethical, and against the rules to demean me in front of them?" As McCrane spoke, he gestured towards the three boys. His tone was as cold as ice, and he seemed to enjoy every minute.

Father Ferran cleared his throat and turned towards the three.

"I want you all to go to your rooms and get cleaned up. I'll send Brother Patrick up in a few minutes to tend to your injuries."

The three quickly turned and almost broke into a run. Tony could feel the warmth of the blood as it oozed from his eyebrow to the bridge of his nose.

"How bad is it?" he asked Dominick.

"It's not too bad. Just a little cut."

"What about my lip?" Robert asked. He could feel the blood drip to his chin.

"It may have to be amputated," laughed Dominick.

"Don't make me laugh," smiled Tony. "I really don't want to laugh."

TWENTY-FIVE

The holidays came and went without much incident. It was the end of March 1960. In spite of the occasional run-in with both Coffer and McCrane, Tony's life at Augustinian Academy was close to being normal.

He wandered through the quiet halls on his way to the chapel. It was Saint Patrick's Day and there were no classes. Tony's festive mood had grown all morning.

"Hello, Father Ferran," Tony said as he entered the church.

"Good morning, Tony. Let's see how we can honor Saint Pat."

While setting up the vestments for the morning mass, Father Ferran told Tony to use as much green in the vestments as he wanted. Tony laughed.

Smiling, Father Ferran walked into the sacristy. Stepping into the room, however, the smile faltered. He rubbed his forehead with his right hand. Tony instinctively knew that something was wrong.

"I need to talk to you, Tony," Father Ferran said, very softly. "I'm afraid I have some bad news."

Tony came over; panic began to fill his body.

"You had better sit down," Father Ferran insisted. He then pulled a chair close to Tony.

"What is it, Father?" Tony spoke in a trembling voice, slowly sitting.

Father John Ferran pulled up a chair and placed it directly across from Tony. He then held both of Tony's hands.

"Our dear friend, Bishop Peter Paul," Father Ferran spoke slowly and softly, "is now with God in heaven."

"He's..." The words were stuck in Tony's throat. "You mean..." Tony could barely force himself to speak. "What are you saying, Father?" The floodgates broke. Tears flowed down his face freely. His hands were trembling in the priest's strong grip. His stomach tightened. His sobs gave way to heaves. Through the blur of his panic and pain, he looked into Father Ferran's eyes. He was telling the truth and it was painful.

"Please, Father! I beg you, please." The young sacristan's sobs took on a gurgling sound. He tried to stand, but he only stumbled.

Father John Ferran gently raised the young seminarian to his feet and took him to the sofa. This kind and gentle principal then got down on one knee and embraced his pupil. In the midst of Tony's cries of anguish, Father John Ferran gave the young seminarian the most precious of all gifts. He cried with him.

The principal held the young candidate for about thirty minutes as they both let their grief come pouring out.

"I'll walk you to your room," said Father Ferran. "You need to rest and grieve."

"I can't," said Tony. His eyes were filled with panic. "I have to finish. You have to say mass. We have to..." his voice cracked. He swallowed hard. "We have to talk to God, Father. He has to give us an answer!"

The tears, the sobbing and the dripping of sweat returned. Tony went to one knee. His entire body began to shake into a near convulsion. It was at that instant that Dominick stepped into the sanctuary.

"I heard yelling..." Dominick started to say, but abruptly stopped.

"Tony, what's wrong?" His cries got louder as he looked towards the principal. "Father! My God, Father! What's happened?"

"Just get the gurney!" Father Ferran's words were firm and crisp, but compassionate. "I'll explain later. We have to get him to the infirmary right now."

Within 90 seconds Dominick was running at full speed returning with the green gurney. Its wheels were screeching. It needed oil.

As they wheeled Tony into the infirmary, he was grasping his stomach. He was also doubled up in pain.

"Get Father Haley. He's in his room," Father Ferran called to Dominick.

It was less than 110 seconds when Dominick turned the corner of the hallway, nearly flying down the corridor with Father Albert Haley in tow, towards the infirmary.

In addition to receiving his PhD in theology, Father Albert Haley had also completed his doctorate in medicine. He was one of the few Catholic priests who was also a board certified medical doctor.

"What is it, John?" Father Haley's voice was panicking. "Dominick said you needed me right away. I thought you were dying."

"I'm fine," answered Father Ferran. "It's Tony who needs your immediate attention. I think he's going into shock, Al."

Father Dr. Haley immediately went to work. "I think you are right!" Father Haley immediately checked Tony's vitals. He then went to the medicine cabinet and unlocked it. He then attached a needle to a syringe and inserted it into the rubber cap of a vial of clear liquid. He slowly drew the liquid into the syringe.

"Get his sleeve rolled up above his bicep," Father Haley directed.

"It's me, Tony," Dominick whispered. "The doctor's here. You're going to be okay."

Father Haley inserted the needle into the bicep of Tony's right arm. He then slowly injected the clear fluid into his muscle.

"Tony. Tony, can you hear me?" Asked Father Haley. "Just nod, if you can."

Tony nodded.

"I've given you a sedative. Just let it work. Just relax and let yourself fall asleep. I'll be taking care of you."

Tony nodded again, but this time he barely moved his head. He felt a slight tingling towards the back of his brain. His feet were feeling numb. The medicine took hold and everything went black.

Father John Ferran then explained the entire incident to both Dominick and Father Haley. Upon hearing of the death of Bishop Peter Paul, Dominick broke down in tears. Father Haley put his arm around the young man.

"Father Peter Paul is the reason I came to the Academy," Father Haley said in a raspy tone. "I met him on a plane from Italy when he was escaping from Germany." Dr. Haley's eyes were welling up. "He was such a kind and compassionate man. He seemed to know your problems before you knew them yourself."

Father Ferran handed the doctor his handkerchief. Father Haley nodded and accepted it.

"Thank you, John." Father Haley then asked, "How did he die? What was the cause of death?"

"A massive heart attack," the principal answered. "That's all I know. Cardinal Spellman called me early this morning and told me. He said he would call me later this afternoon when he finds out about the arrangements."

"What about the prior? What did he say when he found out?"

"I haven't seen the prior," Father Ferran answered. "I tried knocking on his door for a long time, but he never answered." The principal then turned his head away as if to hide a secret. "The prior's been sleeping in a lot later each day. He rarely does morning mass anymore. He doesn't even come into his office until 11:00 a.m. or 11:30 a.m. I'm a little worried about him."

"He's probably nursing a hangover;" Dominick inadvertently said.

Both priests looked at him, taken back. Father Doctor Albert Haley was the first to respond. "The kid might be right." He then tried to muffle his laugh.

Father John Ferran, the school principal, covered his mouth. They both turned away from Dominick and Tony and walked to the far side of the infirmary. Both shook from their concealed laughter.

TWENTY-SIX

The news of the former prior's death sent shock waves throughout the school and the Catholic community. All but two mourned the loss of Bishop Peter Paul. Those two, who actually relished the news, were the present prior and the present vice principal. Based upon the request of Principal Father John Ferran, Monsignor Coffer agreed to have a day of mourning for the former director of Augustinian Academy.

That afternoon a local television news station showed up to get the Academy's response to the death of its former director. Monsignor Coffer had the reporter and crew ushered into his office.

"I never met the man," Monsignor Coffer told the reporter, doing his best to appear to be saddened by the news. "I, however, deeply admire all who held this position before me."

"Since he died in Germany, in the monastery of Ettal, will you attempt to petition your friends there to have his body flown here for burial?" the reporter asked Coffer.

Coffer quickly glanced at McCrane, who was standing in the back. McCrane shook his head, urging Coffer to say no.

"I have never been to Ettal," Coffer answered. "I really would not know who to petition."

The reporter looked surprised.

"Will you then have a memorial service for the late Academy director?" the reporter asked.

"Bishop Peter Paul was a man loved by the Church and respected by the community." Monsignor John Coffer was truly blessed with a velvet voice. He was so articulate that he could have easily been a major challenge in any political race. "Since I do not want to interfere with whatever plans, if any, the Catholic Church may have for the late Peter Paul, I will seek the guidance of the Bishop of our Archdiocese to determine if a memorial is in order. I, however, have made a personal decision to have a day of mourning for the late Bishop here at Augustinian Academy."

"Did you discuss this with the Bishop, the Archbishop, or even Cardinal Spellman?" the reporter asked.

Monsignor Coffer was not sure if the reporter's question was intended to be sarcastic or not. To be safe, he simply turned his gaze directly to the camera. He then put forth his most credible look of both melancholy and sadness.

"I made this decision without consulting with anyone and without any advice from anyone. I truly do know just how hard this job can be since I am now attempting to fill Bishop Paul's shoes. We will have a day of mourning for the former director of Augustinian Academy. I know that it is something that he would have wanted and it is something the students and community need. If I am wrong in my decision to honor the work of this great man, then I stand guilty as charged!"

His speech was brilliant. If he were eligible, he would have been the undisputed winner of an Academy Award. Father Michael McCrane was so impressed, he actually started to clap. The reporter's sharp glance in McCrane's direction, however, limited his enthusiasm to a single clap.

Tony later learned that Bishop Peter Paul had his heart attack while joyously working in the vineyards of his beloved Ettal. The young seminarian's heart skipped a beat, as he thought about this beloved man of God working in a place he once described as one step from heaven. Tony knew that being with God in heaven was indescribable joy, but his earthly emotions caused him to truly miss his longtime friend. Tony began to cry once more.

"I'm so sorry!" Dominick said, as he gently put his hands on the back of Tony's shoulders. "Is there anything I can do to help you?"

Tony looked up at his precious friend.

"Yes, there is." Tony nodded. "You can sit with me for a while. I don't want to be alone."

"Of course, I will." Dominick quietly sat next to Tony that early March day in the open field of Augustinian Academy. They said nothing to each other. They only cried with each other, and they felt the embrace of the Lord, Jesus Christ, comforting them.

Both Tony and Dom were still sitting on the hill overlooking the ball field when Robert came rushing over.

"I've been looking all over for you guys." Robert sounded as if were out of breath.

"If I told you that you were hallucinating and we really were not here, would you continue to look for us?" Dominick asked.

"Come on, Dom," Tony spoke with complete sincerity, "Be nice to him, at least for my sake."

"Okay! For your sake, I will."

"Tony, I wanted to let you know that I was real sorry to hear about Bishop Paul's death," Robert said.

"That is very dear of you, Robert," Tony answered. "Every time he talked about you, he talked about the innocence of your soul. He was genuinely very fond of you."

"Thank you! That means a lot to me."

Tony looked up at Robert and could see a tear running down his cheek. The young seminarian instinctively stood up and embraced Robert. In that instant, tears flooded from Robert's eyes and sobs shook his entire body. Dominick also rose to his feet and put his arms around both of them.

"We may as well make it a group hug," Dominick said.

"Dom, if you turn this moment into a joke, I swear that I'm going to throw you off this hill," Tony said.

Not another word was said. All three quietly turned and started walking towards the dining room for their evening meal.

As they and the other postulants entered the dining hall, they were surprised to see Brother Patrick setting up the television at the entrance to the room.

"What's going on?" Dominick asked Sean Walsh, the dean.

"The prior wants us to see a special news broadcast. I think it has to do with Bishop Peter Paul's death."

Prior to the evening meal, Monsignor Coffer announced to the students that he was going to break with tradition and allow them to watch the evening news.

"Since I realized that all of you, except for the freshmen, knew Titular Bishop Peter Paul, I have decided to allow you to watch this particular news report, which references his death." Coffer then motioned to Brother Patrick to turn on the television set.

"Why did he call him 'Titular Bishop?'" Robert ask Tony.

"I think that he believes that Monsignor Peter Paul was appointed 'Titular Bishop,' which means a bishop in title only, instead of being appointed as a real bishop," Tony answered.

"Well, was he?" Dominick asked.

"I know he wasn't," Tony answered firmly. "Remember, I saw and translated the papal order myself. I really think that Coffer is very jealous and would want to erase the memory of Bishop Peter Paul if he could."

"Why do you think he wants to do that?" asked Ryan. "Did he have some kind of run in with Bishop Paul?"

"I don't know," answered Tony. "I sent the Bishop a letter awhile back and asked him if he knew Monsignor John Coffer, who claimed to be from Germany. I did not receive an answer; but I suppose he did not get a chance to..." Tony's voice cracked and he choked.

Dominick put his hand on Tony's shoulder. "That's okay." Dominick's voice was soft and soothing. "We don't have to talk about this now."

It was nearly 25 minutes before the news anchor announced, "Up next: the report of Bishop Paul's death." Coffer's face was already flushed from both embarrassment and anger, having had to wait so long for the report.

"The death of a true war hero sends both sadness and shock throughout the Catholic community," the television anchor voice said. "Our correspondent Josh Derek has the full story."

The camera cut to a young reporter standing in front of Augustinian Academy.

"Thank you, Allan," the reporter began. "Bishop Peter Paul, the late director of Augustinian Academy, which you see behind me, died yesterday at 10:00 a.m. Eastern Standard Time, of a massive heart attack at the Monastery of Ettal, which is eighty miles from Munich, Germany. The bishop, who was referred to as a 'titular bishop' by Monsignor John Coffer, received the Civilian Medal of Valor in 1946 from then President Harry S. Truman. He was awarded this highest of civilian honors for his work with Dietrich Bonhoeffer in the rescue of thousands of Jews from the clutches of the Nazis. Bishop Peter Paul himself was rescued by now Cardinal Francis

J. Spellman, who was Military Vicar to the Armed Forces at that time. We will now show you our interview with Cardinal Spellman."

Coffer's eyes were glued to the television set. McCrane, who also seemed mesmerized by the report, sat next to him.

"Did you know any of this stuff about Peter Paul and Spellman?" Coffer whispered to McCrane.

"I'm hearing this for the first time."

"Thank you for taking time out of your busy schedule, your eminence, in order to speak to us," the reporter said.

"Peter Paul was a great man," Spellman answered. "I am both humbled and honored to be here talking about him."

"Can you tell us a little bit about the man?"

"I'll do my best," Spellman reflected. "I was contacted by Cardinal Michael Faulhaber, the then Archbishop of Germany, shortly before the fall of Germany in World War II. Cardinal Faulhaber asked for my assistance, as Vicar of the Armed Forces, to have Bishop Peter Paul safely brought to the United States since his life might still be in danger if he stayed at Ettal."

"For the sake of our viewers who do not know about Ettal," the reporter said, "please tell us what it is."

"Of course!" the Cardinal answered. "It is a Benedictine Monastery, just outside of Munich. It was the primary transfer point used by both Father Paul and noted martyr Dietrich Bonhoeffer to safely transport Jews from Germany to the United States."

"Bishop Peter Paul was responsible for the rescue of how many members of the Jewish faith?"

"Eight thousand six hundred and seventeen Jewish lives were saved because of the courage of Dietrich Bonhoeffer and Bishop Peter Paul!" Cardinal Spellman answered.

The entire room of seminarians and priests gasped at the number.

"Now I see why he got the Medal of Valor," the reporter said. "Will you be attending his funeral?"

"I absolutely will be attending his funeral," the Cardinal answered.

"Can you give us the details?"

"I am going to leave that up to his close friend and unsung hero who helped Bishop Peter Paul in Ettal, Monsignor John Coffer. Monsignor Coffer is now the Director of Augustinian Academy on Staten Island. He took the Bishop's place after he retired to Ettal."

"Who recommended Monsignor Coffer for the job?" the reporter asked.

"I don't mind telling you, Josh," the Cardinal said with a smile. "I felt that a person who held the same beliefs and philosophy as Bishop Peter Paul should be the person to take his place. I knew from Cardinal Faulhaber that Monsignor Coffer was also in danger because he was the primary one who helped Bishop Paul and Dietrich Bonhoeffer."

"Can you explain the relationship between Monsignor Coffer and Bishop Paul?"

"Approximately six months after Cardinal Faulhaber asked me to help bring Father Paul to the United States for his safety, he asked me to help someone else." The Cardinal paused for effect. "That person was Father Coffer. When I asked Cardinal Faulhaber if he was doing the same thing that Father Paul was doing, he answered in the affirmative. I then asked him to give me a complete write-up on Father Coffer so the president could award him the Medal of Valor. He told me that Father Coffee was very modest and would choose not to have any publicity. I told him that I understood."

"Then the arrangements for Monsignor Paul will be made by Monsignor Coffer?" the reporter asked.

"That's correct," Spellman answered. "I'm sure he has already contacted his friends in Ettal. Then he will contact me, and I'll approve whatever he wants."

The camera then cut back to the reporter, Josh Derek, who still stood in front of Augustinian Academy.

"We have another interview with Monsignor Coffer," the reporter announced, his face puzzled. "We, however, will not air that tonight, since it is somewhat confusing."

"What is the problem with the interview?" the anchor asked.

"Well, Allan, there seems to be some contradictions in the interview," the reporter said. "As you heard, Cardinal Spellman stated very clearly that Monsignor John Coffer was a close friend of Monsignor Paul. He also said that they worked together in Ettal in the rescue of Jews from the Nazis."

"That's correct Josh. That is what he said."

"In my interview with Monsignor Coffer, he states that he has never met Monsignor Paul, and he has never been to Ettal."

"What?" asked the anchor a bit abruptly, stunned. "Is he calling the Cardinal a liar?"

All eyes in the dining hall were now on Coffer. Monsignor Coffer was now white as a ghost. The blood had completely drained from his face. He then tilted slightly to the right before he fell to the floor with a loud thud.

"Oh my God!" McCrane exclaimed. "Is he dead?"

"No!" Father Ferran held up the Monsignor's head and dabbed his face with cold water. "After that report, I'm sure he wishes he were dead, but he has just fainted."

TWENTY-SEVEN

The next couple of weeks resulted in Monsignor John Coffer spending more time in Cardinal Francis J. Spellman's office than his own.

"The best part," Tony told Dom, "is that he takes McCrane with him. I feel like I've been given a new lease on freedom."

"Do you realize that it's been two weeks since we have laid eyes on either one of them?" Dom asked.

"I haven't even heard them in Monsignor Coffer's quarters." As soon as Tony said it, he bit his lip, wanting to take the words back.

Dominick stopped dead in his tracks. He turned towards Tony.

"What do you mean by heard them in his quarters?"

Tony simply hung his head in shame. Pure guilt oozed from every part of his being.

"I didn't mean anything by it, Dom." Tony gave a deep and remorseful sigh. "I said it by mistake. I lied to you that day I said that Coffer and McCrane were planning to get rid of me. I did hear them say it, but they were not just outside the door. Come with me, I have to show you something."

Tony showed Dominick the secret hearing plug in the vestibule of the school chapel. He then explained to him how it was connected to the Monsignor's quarters and allowed him to eavesdrop on his conversations.

"Please don't judge me," Tony asked Dominick. "I know it's a sin."

Dominick only laughed.

"It's not a sin!" Dominick replied. "In fact, I think God is the one who put it there."

Dominick slowly lifted the plug in and out as if he had found a new toy.

"This is so neat," Dominick laughed. "How long have you known about this?"

"A few months."

"A few months! Why didn't you tell me?"

"I was scared. I didn't want anybody to know. Besides, I knew I was committing a sin. I even had to watch my words when I confessed it in the confessional."

"I bet that got tricky." Dominick laughed. "You must have really had to put a spin on that one. By the way, how did you know you weren't confessing to either McCrane or Coffer?"

"Remember, I'm the sacristan," Tony answered. "I set up the confessionals prior to confessions."

Dominick nodded in approval. He then gently put his hand on Tony's shoulder.

"That just proves my point." He smiled at Tony. "God did this. He even gave you a way out."

"Thanks, Dom." Tony was somewhat relieved. "I just can't figure those two out. This at least gives me some idea as to what they are planning."

"I really do understand," Dominick said. "You have been stressed to the limit. They've been gone for a couple of weeks, and they'll probably be gone a lot longer. That should give you some relief."

"You're right," Tony acknowledged. "I am beginning to feel a lot better."

"I have an idea." Dominick smiled.

Tony was reluctant to ask because it usually meant that someone was going to be the butt of one of Dominick's practical jokes. That butt was usually Robert Ryan.

"We need to pull a good old fashioned practical joke on Robert."

"I knew it," Tony shouted. "I knew that that was exactly what you were going to say."

"So, you disapprove?" Dominick asked.

"No! Of course not! I just knew what you were going to say. I'm completely in!"

"Great!" Dominick announced, throwing up his right arm. "I know the perfect day."

Tony could see the sparkle in Dominick's eyes. Again, he knew exactly what his close friend was thinking. Then they both exclaimed at the exact same time.

"April Fool's Day!"

TWENTY-EIGHT

"Benedecamus Domino!" the voice said as a hand knocked on Dominick Julianno's door.

"Deo gratias!" Dominick answered, in spite of the fact that he had been up for at least half an hour.

It was Friday, April 1, 1960. April Fool's Day. Dominick had been anticipating this for a week. He and Tony would help the Academy to finally return to the days of laughter and humor. A time before Coffer and McCrane.

It was during breakfast that Dominick and Tony told Robert that they had to get something from their rooms for class and they probably would be late for their first class. They asked Robert to save their seats next to him at the table in the chemistry classroom.

"Don't you think you should clear it with Father Ferran first, since he is the teacher?" Robert asked.

"We already have," Dominick lied. "He knows what we are doing."

"Okay," Robert said, "I'll save your seats."

As Tony and Dominick rushed up the stairs from the hall that adjoined the dining area, they failed to see Father Michael McCrane coming down the hall from the main staircase.

"I wonder what those two are up to," he muttered.

Entering the dining hall, he cornered Robert, who was still eating breakfast.

"Didn't your two friends like the food?" McCrane asked.

"What do you mean?" Robert asked, visibly confused.

"Where are Saleem and Julianno?" McCrane asked in a frustrated tone.

"They went to their rooms to get some stuff for chemistry class." Robert's voice began to crack. "Father Ferran knows about it."

"Do I scare you, Robert?" McCrane said with a sarcastic smile across his face.

"Yes, Father, you do!"

"Good!" McCrane responded. "Let's keep it that way."

McCrane then turned and walked towards the head table to join the other faculty members and the dean.

"That man is pure evil," Robert said to the seminarian seated next to him.

Father McCrane sat in the chair next to Father Ferran's. The server immediately placed a plate of scrambled eggs, bacon, and some toast in front of him.

"Can I get you some coffee and juice?"

"Just coffee," McCrane answered.

174

"I understand you sent Saleem and Julianno up to their rooms to get something for your class?" McCrane asked Ferran.

"What are you talking about, Michael?" Ferran said in a confused voice.

"Didn't you authorize them to leave the dining hall early?"

"They don't need authorization from anybody, but they did not do it for me or my class. What is this about?" Ferran was getting irritated.

"I'm not sure." McCrane rose from the table. "But I certainly intend to find out."

In another part of the building, Dominick was whispering fiercely as he directed the Joke of the Century.

"Make sure you grab the fire extinguisher," Dominick told Tony.

"I've already got it." Tony grinned.

"You're on the ball!" Dominick gave Tony the high sign.

They had already managed to move every piece of furniture and clothing in Robert Ryan's room to their own rooms. It was a completely empty room. They then proceeded to fill the room with foam from the fire extinguisher. At the very moment that they had finished their masterpiece, they could hear Satan's primary demon behind them.

"Kneel!" the head disciplinarian yelled with a shriek.

Both seminarians immediately fell to their knees.

"What are you two sons of bi—" McCrane stopped in mid-sentence. "What are you two doing?"

"This is all—" Tony started to say.

The strap from McCrane's cincture struck directly against his mouth.

"You bastard!" Dominick screamed.

McCrane quickly struck Dominick across the face three times with his cincture. Blood erupted from his right cheek.

"To tell you the truth, you pieces of crap, I don't care what you were doing! What I do know is that this gives me just cause to have both of your asses expelled from this place!"

Father McCrane stood over the two and gloated. He then turned and stated to walk away.

"What do you...?"Tony's words were again cut short by McCrane's cincture. This time it came across the back of his head, causing a cut on the side of his right ear.

"Just do as I told you, asshole! What part of kneel don't you understand?"

McCrane walked down the hall, whistling and laughing.

Approximately thirty minutes later, Brother Patrick came to the Robert Ryan's room and began to take pictures. It was as if he was photographing a crime scene. He even took photographs of the two seminarians.

"Don't you think you should have us stand up? You could put numbers on our chests like real mug shots?" Dominick sarcastically asked.

"I really don't like doing this," Brother Patrick answered. "Especially for that *thing* that told me to do it. That man isn't a priest. He's evil."

"I'm sorry," Dominic said, feeling guilty about blaming the wrong person.

"Don't worry about it, Dominick. Did he do this to you?" Brother Patrick pointed to Dominick's left cheek.

Dominick nodded and motioned towards Tony's ear.

"My God!' Brother Patrick said in disgust. "That man is nothing but a butcher and a child abuser. I'll get the first aid kit from my office downstairs. Then I'll be back to take care of this."

"Can't we just go with you to the infirmary?" Tony asked.

"I wish you could," Brother Patrick answered. "But Monsignor Coffer said that you two were to stay kneeling until Father McCrane himself came to get you. Father Ferran argued that he was the principal, and he wanted to see the two of you. The Monsignor, however, said that he wanted McCrane to handle the whole thing and, as long as he was director, that was the way it would be."

"Thank you anyway, Brother Patrick," Tony said, shaking his head.

"I'll be right back." Brother Patrick headed towards the staircase.

Both Anthony Saleem and Dominick Julianno stayed on their knees until 4:30 p.m. It had been almost nine hours from the time that Father McCrane first told them to kneel until the time that he came to get them.

"I really need to go to the bathroom," Dominick noted.

"I bet you do," McCrane replied. "Go ahead, but only one at a time."

"You go first, Tony," Dominick said. He sounded as if he were insisting.

Tony, looking at Dominick, furrowed his brow. He wasn't sure what Dominick was up to, since they had both been to the bathroom less than an hour earlier. Breaking McCrane's rule of kneeling, they'd decided, would add very little to their already overwhelming problems.

"Well, one of you better go before I force you to piss right where you are," McCrane shouted.

Tony slowly got up, then ran towards the bathroom as if he was in great need of relief.

Dominick smiled at McCrane. He then sat back on his heels. McCrane looked confused.

"You really must not know who I am." Dominick spoke very softly. "I'm sure you don't know anything about my family."

"Do you think I give a crap about how rich your family is?" McCrane responded. "Your family sent you here because they wanted you to be a priest or they wanted you to go to boarding school. In either case, Mr. Julianno, they expect me to discipline you! So don't try to threaten me, you worthless piece of crap!"

"Discipline is one thing," Dominick said, as he continued to smile, "but abuse and molestation is another."

"What do you mean by molestation?" McCrane snarled. "I never touched you like that!"

"I'm going to say you did on numerous occasions. By the time the investigation is over, you'll be long gone, back to the shit-filled hole where you belong." Dominick then gave McCrane the finger.

That was all it took. McCrane turned bright red and his knuckles turned white as he gripped the cincture around his waist.

"You little bastard!" McCrane spat the words out through clenched teeth. He ripped the cincture loose from his cassock.

Dominick only looked up at McCrane and smiled as he said, "Hey asshole! With your cassock open like that, you look like a fat Jewish girl!"

McCrane's rage broke. He lashed across Dominick's face with the metal ring attached to the end of his cincture. He continued lashing as his rage boiled over. Blood was splattering against the floor and walls and covered Dominick's face, the metal ring digging into the flesh of his face and neck.

"What the hell are you doing?" Tony screamed as he rushed out of the bathroom.

Other seminarians filed up the steps, classes having just been dismissed. Many froze in horror, watching this massive priest wildly lashing at the face of Dominick Julianno with what appeared to be a large metallic buckle. Dominick just knelt there and appeared to be in prayer. McCrane continued to scream obscenities. His high-pitched voice evoked the anguished sounds of hell's damned.

"My God! Stop!" Sean Walsh screamed at McCrane. "Have you lost your mind? You're going to kill this child, you butchering bastard!"

McCrane stopped in mid-strike. He turned and looked at Sean. McCrane looked like a wild animal just turned rabid. His eyes were bright red. Sweat poured from his brow. White saliva covered his lips. He slowly lowered the cincture strap.

Father Ferran rushed up and tackled McCrane, slamming him to the marbled floor. When he drew his fist back, Monsignor Coffer grabbed his arm.

"There's no need for violence!" Coffer yelled. "We are supposed to be priests!"

Father John Ferran stood up and turned towards the Monsignor. "Do you not see what this handpicked animal of yours did to that helpless child?"

Coffer turned. He gasped upon seeing Dominick covered in blood. "Clean this child up immediately!" he yelled to Brother Patrick.

"He won't let me," Brother Patrick answered.

"No one is going to touch me!" Dominick screamed. He then turned and squinted at McCrane through blood-covered eyes. "Don't you think he's touched me enough? I want my father. I want to call my father now!"

That really won't be necessary," said Coffer, putting out his hand out to McCrane and helping him to his feet. "I think we can handle this without involving your parents. Father Ferran can arrange for transportation to a hospital if necessary and Father Haley can treat you in the infirmary."

The prior then looked around and saw that the hallway was packed with students, including many of the day students. Then his eyes widened. Numerous parents of the day students were also there.

"Father Ferran," Coffer called out as he looked around for the principal. "Where is Father Ferran?" he asked Sean Walsh.

Sean simply shrugged his shoulders. "I thought I saw him headed towards the stairway, but I'm not sure."

"Someone find the damned principal of this school!" the irritated prior yelled.

"I'm here!" Father Ferran yelled from the back of the crowd, way at the end of the hallway.

"Well, get up here and get hold of Father Haley so we can get the Julianno kid cleaned up." The monsignor spoke with his most authoritative voice.

"I'm sorry, but we can't do that." Father Ferran's voice seemed somewhat sarcastic.

"What are you talking about?" snapped Coffer. "I'm in charge here! You will do what I tell you!"

"His father, Joseph Julianno, said that he does not want anyone to touch his son," Ferran said with a slightly smug tone. "He is coming here in a private helicopter; and he'll be here shortly with his own private doctor."

"What!" yelled Coffer. "Who in the hell called his father!"

A slight smile crossed John Ferran's lips. "I did. It's protocol."

"Fuck protocol!" screamed Coffer.

The parents and students gasped in shock. His face turned multiple shades of red and then it began to turn a pale white as the blood drained from his face.

"I'm going downstairs to wait for Mr. Julianno," he said in a rather beaten voice. "Father Ferran," Coffer's voice was very subdued, almost apologetic. "Please ask these fine parents and their students to return to their homes. Have our seminarians return to their responsibilities."

"Don't worry, Monsignor, I'll take care of it," Father Ferran said. "I'll let you take care of the very important responsibility of meeting Mr. Julianno."

Coffer did not respond to Ferran and his sarcasm. He simply turned towards McCrane. "You got us into this mess, let's see if you can get us out of it. Follow me to my office, right now!"

McCrane slumped his head and shoulders as he began to walk past both Dominick and Tony. With Tony blocking the view of everyone else, Dominick looked up at McCrane as he passed. He smiled and flipped a bird at the school disciplinarian.

McCrane clenched his fist and snarled. Tony immediately reacted.

"Father Ferran! Father Ferran!" Tony screamed. "Father McCrane is cursing and threatening Dominick. I think he's going to try and hurt him again."

Father Ferran rushed from the center of the hallway and grabbed McCrane by the front of his open cassock. He slammed him against the wall. Although McCrane was much larger and taller, Father Ferran was a skilled boxer and wrestler. McCrane realized this very quickly when Ferran tackled him to the marble floor.

"I wasn't doing anything," McCrane said with his hands raised.

Ferran looked up at McCrane. "You're nothing but a disgusting coward and pervert." Father Ferran's voice was cold and harsh. "If you ever lay a hand on one of these boys again," he grabbed McCrane's throat with one hand and pulled him down to his eyelevel. "I will kill you." He then squeezed a little harder until McCrane's eyes began to bulge.

Ferran released his grip; he slapped McCrane gently across the cheek. "Go on now. Your mommy is waiting for you in her office."

TWENTY-NINE

Dominick would not let anyone touch or clean his face. Joseph Julianno, after talking to Father Ferran, rescheduled an extremely important legal meeting with Carl Gambino and told him what happened. His boss, who was actually the Boss, or the *capo*, of the largest and most powerful organized crime family in New York, insisted on coming with him.

"You're talking about Dominick, aren't you? He's the one that's going to be a priest?" Gambino asked.

"Not if they did what Father Ferran said they did to him!" Joseph's words were filled with venom. "I'm sorry, Carlo. I did not mean for any of this to be your concern."

Carlo embraced Joseph. "You are my consigliore. You are my family. If it happens to your family, it happens to me. I will go with you. We will take my helicopter." He then motioned to two of the men in his office. "Get Geno and have him get the chopper ready."

"You got it, boss," one said as they left the office.

"I'll call Father Ferran back and let him know that we'll be there in a couple of hours," Joseph said.

"No," said Carlo. "Tell him we'll be there is less than an hour. Don't let them touch Dominick. We'll bring our own doctor."

Joseph nodded. He then looked at Carlo Gambino, the new head of one the most powerful organized families of all time. His eyes welled up and he mouthed the words, "Thank you, my friend."

Carlo winked and nodded back, mouthing his response: "You're welcome, my brother."

Tony was sitting with Dominick in the director's office when they arrived.

"He would not let us give him medical attention," the monsignor said very apologetically as they stepped into the office. "The principal and vice principal will be joining us shortly."

Joseph Julianno only nodded. He rushed to his son and wrapped his arms around him, whispering in Italian.

"What have they done to you, my son? Who did this?"

"I'm okay, Papa," Dominick answered in his limited Italian. "The one who did this is the vice principal. You will meet him shortly. He will probably lie to you, but I will explain everything when we get home."

"You do not want to come back here do you?" Joseph asked with deep concern in his voice.

"Never!" Dominick answered. He smiled as he said it to keep his true feelings from Coffer.

Joseph then turned to Tony and embraced him.

"You look a little bruised too, my dear one." Joseph's tone was very caring.

"I'll be okay," Tony said. "Thank you for your concern, Mr. Julianno."

"You are like a son to me, Tony," Joseph said as he stroked the bandage over the right side of Tony's lacerated cheek. "Please call me Joseph or better yet, Papa."

"Thank you, Papa Joseph," Tony replied.

"Mr. Julianno, this is Father John Ferran, our principal," the monsignor interrupted.

Joseph Julianno looked at Father Ferran and shook his out stretched hand. He looked past him to the six-foot, five-inch very stern Father Michael McCrane.

"And you are?" Joseph Julianno asked in a tone that could refreeze ice.

"Vice Principal Father Michael McCrane," McCrane said, extending his right hand to Dominick's father.

"And who is the person who struck my son in the face so many times with the metal clasp of a cincture, causing his face to look like a mound of ground beef?" Mr. Julianno asked without even bothering to look at McCrane's hand, much less shake it.

"Joseph," Carlo said very softly. He then spoke in Italian. "You are the lawyer," Gambino said. "It is obvious that this animal behind us is the one who did it. He doesn't even have his cincture on. Either that or he's wearing a dress."

Both Joseph and Dominick immediately giggled. Carlo simply held up his hand. "I think we should have our doctor check out Dominick and Tony, then get the hell out of this God forsaken place."

Joseph nodded. Carlo motioned for the doctor to come forward.

"Before we do anything else," Joseph spoke with both calm and with authority. "I want my two sons, Tony and Dominick, medically checked out."

"Of course," said the prior. "You have my permission——"

"I wasn't asking for your permission!" Joseph Julianno said sharply. "I was simply telling you what we were going to do."

"I'll show the doctor where the infirmary is," Father Ferran said.

"Thank you, Father," Joseph said. "You are a good man."

Father John Ferran escorted the doctor, one of Gambino's men, and the two boys to the school infirmary.

"Now, are you going to tell me who did this——and what you intend to do about it?" Joseph Julianno asked very calmly.

"That's a rather complex question," Coffer said. He waved his hand to the chairs.

"Why don't we all sit down," continued Coffer, "and we can talk about this calmly, and rationally."

"I personally think that Joseph is being, and has been, very calm," Carlo Gambino said. "If it had been my son," continued Gambino, "I think my boat would be packed from stem to stern with a lot of 'holy' shark's bait!"

Joseph touched Gambino's hand and gently shook his head. Gambino nodded and stepped back slightly.

"There is no need to jump to conclusions, gentlemen," the monsignor said as he sat behind his desk. "I'm sure you will completely understand once you hear all of the facts."

But the men's faces before Coffer were cold. In that instant Monsignor John Coffer decided how to handle this embarrassing situation. It was better to sacrifice McCrane than to embarrass himself or the Academy.

"Father Michael McCrane, the school's vice principal, acted on his own, and very recklessly, in the handling of this entire situation!" Coffer said in a very emphatic voice.

McCrane's jaw dropped and he looked at Coffer in total disbelief.

"I—did—not—" McCrane started to say.

"Do not say another word!" Coffer immediately warned McCrane. "Your cowboy-like attitude has caused us and those two young men enough heartache for one day!"

Julianno and Gambino gave each other a puzzled look as they called over Geno, the helicopter pilot, and Sammy Grafino, Gambino's personal body guard. They whispered to them in Italian. Geno immediately walked up to Michael McCrane. He stuck a gun in his back and told him to kneel. Grafino went around Coffer's desk. Pulling a .45 caliber semiautomatic from a shoulder holster, he put the tip of the barrel against Coffer's right temple.

"Okay," said Carlo Gambino, in a surprisingly calm, but sadistic tone. "Somebody is going to tell us the truth, and the other one is going to die."

McCrane immediately vomited; Coffer urinated all over himself.

"Well, at least we have some movement," joked Gambino.

"I think that we need to call the authorities, and I want you to leave this house of God!" Monsignor John Coffer actually sounded like a man of respect and authority. His façade, however, was not properly reinforced to withstand the Gambino crime family.

Carlo Gambino had been given a present by both Tommy Lucchese and Vito Genovese, when appointed the *capo* of his family last year. They did so out of respect for his position since they were both *capos* of their own respective crime families. Genovese got him a nickel-plated .45 caliber semi-automatic handgun, which had his name engraved on a silver plate right on the barrel. Tommy Lucchese gave him a matching nickel-plated silencer. Both were in a beautiful handcrafted cherry wood box.

"Did you remember to bring my box?" asked Carlo.

"It's just outside the office," Grafino said.

Carlo looked at Coffer and smiled. "Excuse me for a second, please." Gambino very calmly stepped outside the office and brought in the cherry wood box. He laid it on Coffer's desk and opened it.

He took out the .45 caliber nickel-plated Colt. He then pulled the magazine from the case and slid it into the bottom of the stock. With a single motion he held the slide, moved it back and let it slide forward, loading the bullet into the barrel and pulling the hammer into a cocked position.

John Coffer was not feeling very authoritative or brave anymore; he looked on with total fear.

Gambino looked at him and smiled. He then reached into the case and lifted out a cylindrical tube with a screw-in bolt attached to a rear end cap. The cylinder had numerous baffles on the inside used to diminish sound. It was silver in color. Carlo looked back at Joseph.

"You remember, don't you?"

Joseph smiled and nodded. "Lucchese and Genovese. They got you the gun and silencer to match. It was their tribute. Of course I remember."

"That's right!" laughed Gambino as he screwed the silencer into the Colt 45.

He then looked directly at Coffer and pointed the gun at his forehead. Coffer was so pale that he appeared to be dead. When Grafino touched his head, Coffer convulsed and threw his hands in front of his face.

Gambino laughed. "Hey, tough guy!" Gambino spoke very softly. "Look at me."

Coffer put down his hands and looked directly at Carlo Gambino.

"Are you afraid of dying?" Gambino asked Coffer.

"Of course I am!" Tears were streaming down Coffer's face.

Gambino lowered his gun from Coffer's head to Coffer's groin. "I don't suppose you'll be using those anymore." He then pulled the trigger. It sounded like a cap pistol.

Coffer felt the bullet burn just below the head of his penis, as it sliced into the cushion of his chair.

"Ach mein Gott!" Coffer yelled in German. He then crapped all over himself. Tears flowed freely from his eyes. "I don't want to die," he repeated numerous times.

"The entire matter should have been turned over to the principal, Father Ferran. He should have been the one who dealt with it," the Monsignor answered as he sobbed. "Father Ferran has the experience to deal with these boys. Father McCrane does not. It is that simple. I intend to fully discipline Father McCrane for his wrongful actions. I attempted to make sure that both seminarians received the best medical attention that there is, but your son refused any medical help at all. I suppose because of his personal anger towards Father McCrane and, personally, I do not blame him! Michael is a harsh disciplinarian, almost sadistic at times."

Gambino's head shook. Coffer was encouraging them to kill McCrane.

"He should not have ever struck your son or Tony," Coffer went on, "especially not with the ring of the cincture. That was demonic. He was acting out of rage. I give you my word, as the prior of this seminary, that he will be punished."

McCrane, as he listened on, seethed with fury. He bit his lip and his face became a bright red. The veins in his neck were bulging and throbbing.

"Hey, Boss," said Geno. "This guy's about ready to burst an artery."

"It would save us a lot of trouble if he did," Gambino said. He put his matching 45 and silencer back into the cherry wood case and gave it to Grafino. He then told him to get the boys and the doctor.

"Well, it's getting late." Joseph Julianno rose from his chair. "I suppose that is all of the information that you are going to give us, and I'm sure that very little of it is true." He turned towards the kneeling McCrane and motioned to Geno, who put the gun back in his pocket.

"Stand up," he said to McCrane. "You like to beat helpless little boys, don't you?"

"None of that is true—"

The gun was placed into his back again.

"Look closely at my face," Joseph emphasized. "You'll see it soon and you will remember it. You cowardly bastard."

The boys and Father Ferran returned. The doctor said that they would be fine. They had to receive some shots and stitches. Tony would be fine in a couple of days, but it would take Dominick a little longer to completely heal.

"I'll check on him at your house in the next couple of days," the doctor said.

"Thank you so much," Joseph said as he shook the doctor's hand.

"I don't understand. Are you pulling Dominick out of school?" the monsignor asked.

"No!" Julianno answered. "I'm not pulling him out of school. I'm pulling him out of this place. I'll get him tutors and he'll go to school in New York. He'll have a fine education—without being beaten up by his worthless vice principal!"

190

Joseph Julianno turned his back on the monsignor and looked directly at Dominick.

"Is that okay with you, son?"

Dominick vigorously nodded.

"What about Tony?" Dominick asked.

"Tony, you are welcome to come with us. I would be honored to get tutors for you also. I'm sure I can explain to you parents. Or I can arrange to get you in the finest school in Jacksonville, Florida. It is completely up to you, my son."

"I'm truly honored, Mr. Julianno." Tony answered. "I need to stay here and at least try to become a priest. Anything other than that would cause my mother and father a great deal of heartache."

"You are a caring and brave young man." Joseph Julianno caressed the bandage on Tony's face. "You deserve to become a priest, and you deserve better than this."

Within a half hour everyone had left, and Tony found himself alone with monsignor Coffer. The director sat behind his desk and leaned back in his black leather chair. He sat quietly for several minutes, staring directly at Tony, attempting to intimidate the young seminarian. Tony stared back. It was in that moment that he could clearly see that Coffer was not only a liar and evil—he saw something else too, but something out of place. Monsignor John Coffer was afraid. Tony was not sure if he were afraid of him or Dominick's father. In either case, he appeared to be very frightened. In fact, deathly frightened. That was when he noticed the smell.

"It smells like someone crapped in here," Tony noted.

The Monsignor reached between his legs and touched the bullet hole in the cushion of the chair. It was then that the smell of his own urine and feces attacked his nostrils. He put his hands over his nose and mouth to cover his embarrassment.

"It's late," the monsignor said to Tony. "I'll have Sean Walsh pick someone else to be the sacristan for tomorrow morning's mass. That will give you a little more sleep. I do want to see you, however, right after breakfast tomorrow morning. At that time, I'll decide what to do with you. You are dismissed to go to your room now. Remember, it is magnum silentium."

Tony stood up and felt very dizzy. The reason came to him very suddenly.

"Monsignor, I haven't had anything to eat since breakfast this morning."

"Don't you think I know that?" Coffer snapped. "A little fasting is always good for the soul! Now, get to your damn room!"

Tony quickly turned and left. When Tony opened the door to his room, however, there was a large brown bag sitting in the chair by his desk. A note was attached to the bag. It read: *Sister Gertrude and I put this together for you. We knew you would be hungry after such a busy day. Please remember that Sister Gertrude and I, and God will always love you, no matter what.*

It was signed by Robert Ryan. Robert also added a postscript in which he told Tony that he had gotten all of his stuff back. He went on to say that he thought that it would have been a great practical joke, had McCrane let them finish it.

The bag contained two ham and cheese sandwiches, a bag of chips, a Styrofoam cup full of milk, and a small bowl of cherries. Robert knew how much Tony loved cherries, and now Sister Gertrude also knew. Tears welled up in Tony's eyes as he sat to eat this very special meal. Once he had finished he simply lay on his bed and cried like a baby.

THIRTY

"Benedecamus Domino!"

"Deo gratias!" Tony answered that Saturday morning of April 2, 1960. Tony truly believed that this would be the most important day of his life. It would determine the path he would take and the very reason for his existence.

If he had only known that this would be the last meal he would have with his friends, he would have been a lot more pleasant. He also would not have finished his meal so quickly. He would regret this for years to come. He already missed Dominick, wondering if he would ever see him again. Robert Ryan, too, truly was a dear friend. He embraced Tony at the breakfast table and laughed about the practical joke.

"I don't see why they are making such a big deal out of it," Robert said. "It was just a simple prank."

Tony nodded and gave a halfhearted smile.

"Thank you, Robert, for the food. I really was hungry."

"You're very welcome. It was actually Sister Gertrude's idea," Robert answered. "She seemed to know that you had not eaten all day."

Tony smiled in appreciation. "Well, I have to go to find out my fate from the prior."

"Please let me know his decision as soon as you can." Robert said. "Please, don't do like Dominick and leave me."

Tony only smiled, then headed towards the director's office.

"Enter," the monsignor called out as Tony knocked on the open door.

"You said you wanted to see me this morning," Tony said as he entered Coffer's office.

"Come in, Tony. Please have a seat." The monsignor seemed in a surprisingly jovial mood. Tony wasn't sure as to why he seemed so happy.

"Well, today I'm supposed to determine your fate, aren't I?" Monsignor Coffer looked directly at Tony as he gently stroked his chin.

As soon as the young seminarian looked into Coffer's eyes he knew why he was so jovial. He was relishing the idea of hurting Tony. It was as if he had won some grand prize. He won the right to torture a helpless seminarian and no one could stop him. Evil emanated from his eyes. He was going to do this simply because he could.

"I've been giving this a lot of thought, Mr. Saleem," Coffer said as he leaned in Tony's direction. "In fact, I only had a couple of hours sleep because of my concern for this situation."

"I'm sorry to hear that—"

"Shut up, you worthless piece of crap!" The monsignor spat his venom filled words at Tony. He then rose from behind his desk, walked over to the door to his office, and closed it. "Do not speak again until I give you permission! Do you understand?"

Tony only nodded.

"Well, anyway, this is what I have decided to do." The monsignor returned to his leather-covered chair. "I will probably expel you!"

Tony's heart seemed to suddenly get stuck in his throat. He could tell from looking into Coffer's eyes that he was dead serious.

"The only problem is that it would be very difficult for you to get into another school, since it's so late in the year. Do you agree?"

Tony begged God to give him strength to show no pain or weakness.

"I asked you a question," Coffer said, as he leaned forward. "Did you not hear me, or are you in shock?"

"Neither." Tony spoke in a measured voice. "You told me not to speak again until you gave me permission. I assume that you're giving me permission. I agree that I would have a hard time getting into another school if I was forced to leave now."

"At least we agree on something!" Coffer raised his hands in celebration. "You will stay here until the end of the school year."

Tony waited for the rest of it, but the monsignor then got up from his chair and went towards the door as if he were finished. As he passed Tony, however, the young seminarian could see the sadistic look in this diabolical so-called man-of-the-cloth's eyes.

This is not finished, Tony thought. *In fact, I'm sure it's far from being finished.*

The monsignor stopped at the door. He then put his hand to his forehead.

"I almost forgot." Coffer said. "I've got more for you."

He then looked at Tony and was obviously disappointed when he did not see any change in the young seminarian's stoic demeanor. Tony could see the anger burning in Coffer's eyes.

"You will not associate with any of the other seminarians." The monsignor sounded like a hammer as he pounded in each and every restriction that he was placing on the now terrified seminarian. "You will not wear the traditional cassock and cincture of a postulant," the monsignor continued. "You will dine at a table away from the other seminarians. You will not be allowed to have any activities with the other seminarians. Whenever there is a service of any kind in the chapel you will sit on the last pew in the back. You will only be allowed to have conversations with the teacher while in classes. You will not be allowed to speak to or have any conversations of any type with any of the students, postulants or day students at any time. Do you understand?"

Tony only nodded, desperately trying to hold back his emotions.

"Good!" Coffer said in a frustrated tone. "At the end of this school year, in about three months, I'll evaluate how well you did. I will then make a decision and let you know."

The monsignor scrutinized Tony's eyes, hoping to see the slightest sign of anguish. When he saw none, the anger in his own eyes changed to rage.

"Get the hell out of here and get to your room!" Coffer motioned towards the door.

"Today is Saturday." Tony said. "Do I report to a work detail?"

"No!" Coffer scowled. "You are not part of the routine of this Academy anymore. Just go to your room and stay there!"

Tony turned and walked to his room, where he would spend his first day in complete isolation. He then dropped to his knees. His tears burst forth like a broken dam.

"My life is gone," he whispered. "I've got nothing left. I don't think I can do this!"

It was like a nightmare. The first three days of Tony's complete segregation from the students of Augustinian Academy were far more difficult than he thought.

"I truly do not know how I'm going to make it for sixty-three more days," Tony wrote in his letter to Dominick. "I really do miss you, but I know you made the right decision to leave this place. I wish I could do the same, but my parents would not be as understanding and supportive as your parents. I'm sure my mom would be so heartbroken that it probably would kill her. I'm not sure how my dad would act."

Tony knew that his letter to Dominic was basically the only type of honest communication that he could have with another human being for the remainder of the term. The priests at the academy would barely talk to him and even if they did, he certainly could not be honest with them. He also knew that he absolutely could not be honest with his tormenters, Coffer and McCrane. If nothing else, the next 63 days would teach him how to mask his true feelings and hide behind the persona of whomever he created.

"I'll never let them know how much pain I'm feeling," Tony wrote to Dom. "That's the only weapon I have against them. Watching them get frustrated is the only thing I look forward to these days."

The days became longer and longer and far more agonizing. The young seminarian was convinced that there was no greater punishment than isolating a person, then forgetting about that person. Tony would even look forward to the negative and demeaning contact he had with Father McCrane.

"Even if he humiliates me every time he talks to me," Tony wrote, "it lets me know that somebody is still aware of my existence."

The only bright spot in Tony's days of torment took place on Sunday, April 17, 1960. It was Easter Sunday. A lot of the seminarians had gone home for the Easter holidays. Augustinian Academy was as empty as a tomb. The dining hall, which normally held almost 200 people, was now reduced to fifteen. This included Tony and the few remaining seminarians, as well as some members of the faculty.

Easter Sunday was a special time at Augustinian Academy for those who did not go home for the holidays. Since Mass was not held until 8:30 a.m., they would be allowed to sleep in late. They also would breakfast with the faculty at the faculty dining table at 9:30 a.m. Then they were allowed to feast on a buffet of all kinds of cereals, fruits, waffles, pancakes, eggs, ham, and almost every other imaginable breakfast item. The one element of the whole experience, however, that made it the most memorable of all the things that happened at the Academy was the wine. Each of the remaining seminarians, regardless of their age, were allowed to have a single glass of red wine.

Tony, however, was not allowed to take part in the festivities. He had to sit at the last table in the dining hall, furthest from the faculty table. He also was allowed only a single bowl of oatmeal and a glass of milk. The oatmeal, however, on that Easter Sunday was delivered to him by Sister Gertrude. The aging nun, now 81 years old, came walking into the dining hall from the kitchen. She carried the bowl of oatmeal in one hand, steadying herself with her cane in the other. After she placed the bowl in front of Tony, she went into the pocket of her habit and pulled out a folded napkin. She placed the napkin on the table in front of the oatmeal. She then opened the napkin, revealing a folded note.

Tony gently grasped the precious nun's hand and let a tear fall from his eye to the back of her arm. He had seen what she had done to the oatmeal. A ring of cherries surrounded the edges of the oatmeal, and an outline of the cross made of cherry halves was in the center of the oatmeal. When he looked up at her with tears flowing from his cheeks, he could clearly see that her eyes were also welling up. She quietly moved away and walked slowly back to the kitchen.

After Tony took several bites of his oatmeal and cherries, he opened the note. It appeared to be written by a child or someone who did not know the English language very well. Sister Gertrude had transferred to Augustinian Academy from Germany, the same year that Monsignor Peter Paul was put in charge of the Academy. The note almost caused Tony to openly start weeping.

He has risen! God loves you!

Tony held the note to his heart. He knew that he would treasure it forever. Sister Gertrude entered the dining hall again. This time she was carrying something hidden in the folds of her habit. When she came to the corner of Tony's table, she gently slid the juice glass filled with wine from the folds of her habit to the edge of the bowl of oatmeal. She then smiled with saintly satisfaction, turned and walked back to the kitchen. Tony bowed his head and thanked God for bringing this saintly nun to Augustinian Academy.

The joy and happiness of that Sunday morning, however, was virtually wiped out by the grief and anguish that Tony would experience that evening. He had been cooped up in his room for hours that Easter Sunday, and he wanted some fresh air. Tony decided to take a walk in the outside courtyard. As he came down the side stairway to the first floor, however, he noticed that the light was still on in the kitchen. As he stepped into the kitchen he heard a scrapping sound. He then saw Sister Gertrude on her hands and knees scrubbing the floor with a bucket and small brush. When this angel of God saw him coming, she immediately put her finger to her lips, warning Tony to not say a word.

"You can hold yourself responsible for this, Saleem." Monsignor Coffer's words were cold and bitter as they echoed from Tony's right. "She should have never given you the cherries and especially not the wine!"

The seminarian simply looked at the director, refusing to let his emotions show. He quietly scanned the kitchen in an effort to spot the meat clever. He felt so much hatred and disgust for the demonic being which stood before him that he truly wanted to split his head.

How could anyone do this to an 81-year old nun? Tony, seemingly unaffected, walked away.

"I bet you think you're really tough, you asshole!" Coffer shouted. "Do you think you're impressing this old woman? She's just like you and everyone else that Peter Paul touched! She's worthless!"

Tony opened the door in the center of the hallway and stepped into the courtyard. He slowly walked to the very end of the structure, into the darkness that overlooked the field. He looked around to insure that he was all alone. He then fell to his knees and wept. He sobbed so deeply that his body shook. His pure hatred for John Coffer burned so intensely that it scorched the very essence of his soul.

He was not sure how long he had been kneeling at the edge of the courtyard or when he started walking back to the building. He did know, however, that the sight of precious Sister Gertrude bent over and scrubbing that floor had pushed his faith to the very edge. He had to go to the chapel. As he stepped into the dimly lit room, he saw the votive candles which flickered before the statue of the Virgin Mary. He quietly slid into the first pew and fell to his knees. For the first time in his life, the once enthusiastic seminarian felt very empty. He was completely numb.

"I wonder how many candles I would have to light to bring Monsignor Coffer to justice."

He stuck his hand in his pocket and counted out the three quarters and two dimes.

"Eighty-five cents, I don't think that would buy me ten seconds worth of prayer with anyone in heaven, much less God."

Tony laughed at the absurdity of his own statement. He knew it truly was the basic belief of many Catholics, especially those who lit the candles in front of him. He also knew that the concept was for pure profit. The irrationality of paying ten cents to light a single votive candle, in the belief that the Virgin Mary would carry your request to God, was a mockery to Tony's intelligence.

"When a priest is ordained, he is called *alter Christos*. But this man is the exact opposite of Christ. Jesus would never do that to an 81-year old nun."

As the young seminarian continued to kneel in that chapel, he slowly but surely began to strip away the tenets and doctrines of the Catholic faith from his soul. Nearly an hour had passed when Tony noticed the vestibule door.

"This would be a perfect time."

Tony slowly rose from his knees and quietly stepped into the vestibule. As he fumbled for the plug in the darkness of the room, his hands began to sweat. He slowly lifted it and could hear Coffer and McCrane's voices.

"He said he wants me to meet him." McCrane's voice was strained. "It's at an abandoned church in New Jersey."

"Why in the hell would you even consider meeting him?"

"Didn't you hear me the first time?" McCrane said. "He said he has a film that would be of great interest to me."

"I wouldn't care if he had the original cut of Elmer Gantry." Coffer cleared his throat. "You don't know who this guy is, and you don't know what this is about. I'd tell him to screw himself!"

"There's no way I can do that. I know where the abandoned church is located. I've been there before."

"That's not the point, Michael. This whole thing makes absolutely no sense whatsoever. You have not given me one good reason as to why you're going to drive out to Jersey at this hour of the night and meet some unknown lunatic who has an 'interesting' film."

McCrane spoke slowly and without emotion. "He says that he has the original film of Bonhoeffer's execution."

Tony heard something drop and glass shatter. He quickly looked around, then realized the sound came from Coffer's quarters.

"It's just a broken glass!" Coffer snapped. "I'll get it later." Coffer slowly sat in the chair behind him.

"Do you believe him?" The monsignor's voice cracked.

"He said that Bonhoeffer was hung from a tree and a meat hook was used to hold the noose." McCrane slowly sat in the chair across from Coffer. "He went on to tell me that piano wire was used. Three of the guards turned their heads away, but the leader, whose face can be seen very clearly, was enjoying every second of Bonhoeffer's excruciating death."

Father Michael McCrane leaned forward and looked directly into the monsignor's shocked eyes. "Now does it make sense? Have I given you at least one good reason as to why I have to drive to Jersey?"

John Coffer's face turned pasty white. Beads of sweat formed across his forehead. He barely had the strength to simply nod.

"How do you think...?"

"I don't know!" McCrane interrupted. "But he knows and he obviously has something! I need to find out what it is!"

"I agree." Coffer spoke in a shaky voice. "You do have to meet him. What will you do when you meet him?"

"I'll deal with it!"

"What do you want me to do?"

"Stay here and do what you do best. Get drunk and be the coward you've always been. I'll take care of the dirty work. I always do!"

Tony could hear the sound of metal moving against metal as McCrane slid a .45 caliber round into his semi-automatic handgun.

"What the hell!" Coffer yelled. "You're not going to use that thing are you?"

"That's the difference between you and me. I will use it. As I already said, all you have to do is stay here and be the coward you are."

A few minutes later, Tony could hear the door to Coffer's quarters shut. His hand was trembling as he slid the plug back into place. He had to slowly stand up and take several deep breaths in order to calm his shaking knees and trembling body.

"Who are these people?" Tony left the chapel and slowly walked back to his room.

THIRTY-ONE

"Benedecamus Domino!"

Tony heard the footfalls as they moved from room to room, but they went past his door since no one was allowed to knock on it any more. The movement in the hallway, however, made Tony aware that everyone had returned from the Easter holiday.

I wish I could talk to Dom, Tony thought. *I really would like to get his take on what I heard last night.*

As Tony was putting on his robe to walk to the shower, he was surprised by a knock. He quickly pulled it open. Sean Walsh stood there, a letter in hand. It was morning mail call. He simply handed the letter over. It was from Dominick. Tony quickly shut the door and tore open the envelope.

I really do miss you, Dominick wrote. *I pray for you all the time and worry about how they are treating you. My dad knows Dr. Frank Lucey, whose son, John, is a day hop at the academy. His dad has him call me every day after school and fill me in on what's happening to you. Actually, talking to John has caused me to think about you a lot more. Well, not much, but a little more.*

Tony laughed at that line.

Dominick went on to tell Tony what was happening in his own school, indicating how glad he was not to be at Augustinian Academy. With a tear threatening to well up, Tony read: *The only things I miss are you and Robert.*

The next lines, however, made his pulse race.

"My dad told me this morning that Mr. Gambino, his boss, had found out something about Father McCrane. When I asked him what it was, he told me he couldn't say, but it's very embarrassing. I'll let you know what it is, as soon as I find out."

Tony let the letter fall to his lap. *What did Mr. Gambino know?* Though Tony knew that he'd be late for breakfast, he could not help himself. He had to read the letter one more time.

As Tony sat at his usual table by himself, he looked into the kitchen, hoping to see Sister Gertrude. His heart went out to the elderly nun. He felt both love and sadness for what she had done for him. Her unselfish act of kindness meant more to him than anyone could imagine. The pain she had to suffer because of it brought him to near tears.

That rotten piece of dog waste! Tony thought. *If there really is a God, and if He really is just, then Coffer needs to be in hell!*

Suddenly Father Ferran burst into the dining room. He looked very perplexed, walking at a rapid pace. He went straight to Sean Walsh and whispered in his ear. Sean immediately stood up and tapped a glass to get everyone's attention.

"Father Ferran needs to say something. Please give him your undivided attention," Sean said solemnly.

"I have some very sad and horrifying news." Father John Ferran spoke slowly and deliberately. "We were just notified by the New Jersey State Police of a tragedy. Around four o'clock this morning, they found the body of a person in an abandoned church near Newark. They believe that the body is that of Father Michael McCrane."

The gasp in the room erupted like something from a horror movie. Tony dropped the glass he was holding; it broke beside his feet. All eyes turned towards Tony. He attempted to pick it up, but Sister Gertrude was already there with a rag and a dustpan. She gently touched his hand in an effort to comfort him.

"I know we are all distraught and in shock over this news," Father Ferran continued, "but there is no need to panic. We will all get through this. The monsignor wants all of us to go to chapel and pray. He will join us shortly and tell us what he knows."

As they gathered in the chapel, Tony sat in his usual place in the back pew.

Is he going to tell them about his conversation with McCrane? Tony wondered. *What about McCrane meeting someone at the church where his body was found? What about the film he was supposed to pick up? How did he die? Was he murdered?* Tony was full of questions, but he could not ask them. He would not dare ask them to the only person allowed to speak to him. That person was the biggest question of all.

"I was contacted at about 5:30 this morning by an investigator from the New Jersey State Police, asking if Father Michael McCrane worked here," the Monsignor said. "He went on to tell me that they found identification that belonged to Father McCrane on a body in some abandoned church near Newark. He wanted me to come to the morgue…" The monsignor pulled a handkerchief from his pocket and wiped his eyes. "I felt that it was more important for me to be here to watch over all of you instead of going there to identify the body."

Even from the back of the chapel Tony could immediately tell that Coffer was lying. Even more, he was very scared.

"So, I sent Brother Patrick," Coffer continued. "Brother Patrick called a few minutes ago from the morgue and advised it truly was the body of Father Michael McCrane, our beloved vice principal." Coffer wiped his eyes once more. "I know all of you, along with me, are in complete and total shock over this matter. Since the news media has gotten a hold of this story, I'm afraid that they will air it fairly soon. In order to keep your parents from needlessly worrying about you, I want each and every one of you to use the phones in the office to call them. Let them know that you are okay and you are not effected in any way by this tragedy. This entire event is both dreadful and appalling, but we will get through it. You are dismissed."

Tony could not believe it. Coffer was more concerned about the feelings of the parents than the feelings of the students. This man of God also hadn't mentioned God even once nor offered up a prayer.

He truly is a liar, Tony thought. *There is something deep inside of him that he wants to keep hidden from everyone. I wonder if this has something to do with Dom's letter.*

Since the seminarians were kept secluded from the outside world, they were dependent upon the day hops to hear the full story about Father McCrane. John Lucey personally delivered a newspaper article to Tony.

"Here," John said softly, knowing that he was not supposed to be talking to Tony. "My dad said to give this to you and no one else."

It was a large manila envelope—sealed. It was not until later that afternoon that Tony finally could opened it in the privacy of his room. It contained the newspaper article, which detailed what happened to Father McCrane.

Priest's Body Found Hanging In Abandoned Church! The headline read.

The article went on to state that the police were still investigating the matter, but they needed to wait until the completed autopsy before establishing if the incident was a homicide or a suicide. The fact that the noose was made of piano wire that hung from a meat hook attached to the church rafter caused the police to consider foul play. A ladder, however, was lying on its side beneath the body. An investigator was quoted as saying that this could indicate that the ladder was deliberately kicked away by McCrane as he committed suicide. The police did not say if there was a note, but they did say that an unusual item was found at the scene that might give them some answers.

"They must be talking about the film of Bonhoeffer's execution," Tony murmured. "Those are the same items that McCrane told Coffer about. But none of this makes sense."

Tony's thoughts began to spin. Both Coffer and McCrane could be mass murderers, for all he knew. But why was he involved? He knew absolutely nothing about those two. They had nothing in common. There was no way to connect the dots, since there were no dots which led to him. The only thing that they had in common was Monsignor Peter Paul, and both McCrane and Coffer claimed they never met Peter Paul.

It was not until the afternoon of Wednesday, May 4, 1960, that Father Michael McCrane's death became the focus of the news media once again. It was another week before the secluded seminarians of Augustinian Academy were allowed to view any news reports in regards to the incident. The evening of May 12, 1960, all of the students and staff of Augustinian Academy, as well as the outcast Tony Saleem, gathered together in the auditorium for an informational meeting. The information consisted of a special television report on the death of Father McCrane. The only person who was not there was Monsignor John Coffer.

The report was delivered by Douglas Edwards of CBS evening news.

The news anchor described the death of Michael McCrane as one of the most bizarre stories of the decade. Initially, he repeated the details of how and where McCrane's body was found, including the fact that he was hung from the rafters with piano wire that was attached to a meat hook. Edwards also restated the finding of an "unusual item" at the crime scene.

"CBS News has determined," Edwards said, "that the unusual item of evidence was a film of the graphic execution of theologian Dr. Dietrich Bonhoeffer," Edwards said. "The film is so horrific that CBS has decided not to show it in its entirety. We will, however, show small increments of the film. Those increments are the ones that relate to the McCrane death."

In the first film clip, a badly beaten and crippled man was being forced to hobble from a concrete building along a gravel pathway. The person shooting the film sought to capture the pure pain and anguish that the man was going through.

"The man in the film, who is being tortured, is Dietrich Bonhoeffer," the news anchor said. "He is being forced to walk on broken ankles and feet, which have just been burnt with a blow torch. The actual torture of Bonhoeffer is shown in the earlier portions of the film. It is so graphic and grotesque that even the combat-seasoned SS guards are shown in the film as turning their heads."

As the camera backed away, those who surrounded Bonhoeffer were brought into view. Every single person in the auditorium went into momentary shock. They could not believe what they were seeing.

"The man you see in the forefront," Edwards said, "is the person who has been identifying himself as Father McCrane."

Douglas Edwards paused, allowing the viewers to absorb the full impact of what they heard.

"He is dressed in civilian clothes," Edwards continued, "because he is, in actuality, a Gestapo agent. His true name is Franz Heydrich. It is believed that Heydrich stole the identification papers and passport of Michael McCrane. McCrane was a member of the Augustinian Cannons of Ettal. He and twenty-one of his fellow priests were executed by the Gestapo just one month prior to the end of the war. Bonhoeffer, however, was executed on April 9, 1945, just three weeks prior to the end of the war. It is that execution that you are witnessing now."

"What the hell," Tony said, as he sat alone in the back of the auditorium. Monsignor Coffer knew about this murder, Tony realized.

Tony quickly scanned the people in the auditorium.

"He's not here. I don't see him anywhere," Tony murmured. "If I were innocent, this is exactly where I would be. But he's not here."

Douglas Edwards went on to explain how the police and the Federal Bureau of Investigation were not sure if Heydrich had committed suicide out of remorse, or if he was murdered because of what was on the tape. The investigation was still under way.

"According to sources close to the investigation," Edwards commented, "Cardinal Francis Joseph Spellman had also been interviewed by the FBI. Spellman acknowledged the fact that he did help to bring Franz Heydrich into the United States, believing that he actually was Father Michael McCrane. According to Cardinal Spellman, the late Cardinal Michael von Faulhaber requested that the individual identified as Father Michael McCrane be brought to the United States for his own safety. Cardinal Spellman, who was appointed Vicar of the United States Armed Forces by President Franklin D. Roosevelt, felt that it was his duty to assist Cardinal Faulhaber. Cardinal Michael Faulhaber, of the Archdiocese of Munich, passed away in 1952, at the age of 83."

Edwards went on. In the end, the news report was an hour long. The newscast gave as many details as possible within legal limits. The FBI vowed to resolve the issue, even if they had to interview the Pope himself. Everyone left the auditorium in both absolute silence and complete shock.

THIRTY-TWO

"Benedecamus domino!"

The words rang out the morning of June 10, 1960. It was a very special day for Tony Saleem. It was his last day of the school year—yet hopefully not his last day at Augustinian Academy.

"I did it!" he said aloud. "I did it! I beat him! I did everything he told me. I took everything he had and still survived. He has to let me return, and I won't have to explain anything to Emma."

The day passed very quickly for Tony, despite of the fact that even now, on this last day, he still had to spend it in isolation. The overwhelming humiliation and complete separation from everyone that Tony had to endure for sixty-three days would have broken the average child. Tony, however, was proud of the fact that he had endured it. He knew that the past nine weeks would leave an indelible scar on both his mind and soul. He also knew that if he did come back, he would not return as the same person. Sixty-three days of isolation and torture would change the strongest of men, and even more a teenager.

The tap on his shoulder as he was finishing his lunch startled him.

"I did not mean to scare you."

The voice behind him was soft, but sinister. Tony recognized it immediately.

"What is it, Monsignor?" Tony asked as he looked up with his plastic smile.

"I need to see you in my office," the monsignor paused, "After lunch, of course."

Tony only nodded and continued with his nondescript smile as he turned away to finish his bologna sandwich. Indifference was the only weapon he had and it seemed to be very effective on John Coffer. The prior, noticeably irritated, stomped out of the dining hall. Tony's smile got a little bigger.

"As you know, Mr. Saleem," Coffer said when they were both settled in the office, "you'll be leaving us in the morning."

Tony couldn't help but think how inane Coffer's remarks were. "Are you going to expel me?" Tony then looked directly into Coffer's eyes.

The director became flushed and small beads of sweat formed on his forehead. A drop of sweat formed between his upper lip and nose. He crossed his arms and leaned back in his massive leather chair. Tony already had his answer before Coffer broke eye contact. He knew that the monsignor was about to lie.

"That is a serious problem you have Mr. Saleem. You are rude, and you have a tendency to show disrespect to those in authority. I truly do not know what I am going to do with you. Does that answer your question?"

At that very moment, Tony had the last vestiges of his faith stripped from his soul. He knew that if there truly were a God and a Satan, then the thing that sat behind that cherry wood desk was the essence of Satan dressed in Godlike clothing. He felt no need to maintain any semblance of respect for it.

"No," Tony said, locking in on Coffer's eyes. "It really does not answer my question. But that is what you do best, isn't it?"

The monsignor's eyes widened and his right hand began to noticeably shake. Tony could clearly see the mixture of rage and confusion building up in his eyes.

"You love to use your velvet voice to spread deception and confusion," Tony continued. "You would sooner lie, even if the truth would suit you better."

"You God d—"

"How does a man," Tony interrupted Coffer mid-curse, "who is supposed to be an *alter Christos* use the Lord's name in vain so easily. Your ability to use such blasphemous and filthy language causes me to wonder if you are even a priest!"

It was as if Tony Saleem had slammed a stake directly through John Coffer's heart.

Coffer's face turned pasty white. The furious rage in his eyes turned to absolute fear. He cowered back to the safety of his leather chair, and brought his left hand to his mouth, as if to hide his emotions. It was in that instant Tony knew that he had his prey locked into the crosshairs of his scope. He pulled the trigger.

"You are no different than Father Michael McCrane. I mean Franz Heydrich." Tony smiled as Coffer continued to burn. "You are both despicable imposters. Just who in the hell are you? I personally think that you are nothing more than a piece of Satan's own defecation, which has come out of the slime of this earth."

By this time Tony was standing almost directly in front of Coffer's massive desk. This entire event was so unexpected that the Monsignor did not know how to react. He simply sat in seemingly catatonic shock. Once again his eyes revealed his change from unmitigated fear to full-blown panic. Tony then delivered the final fatal blow. He turned and walked out of the room, without giving him a chance to respond.

Everything was packed. Dominick's chauffer had already placed Tony's belongings in the back of the limousine. Both Tony and the Julianno family had a prearranged agreement that the driver would be there between 1:00 p.m. and 2:00 p.m. Tony deliberately timed his meeting with Coffer to occur within that time period. As Tony calmly walked down the hall from the director's office towards the main entrance, Coffer stormed after him.

"Don't you dare walk out of my office without my permission!" Coffer shrieked.

At the sound of voices, a few people began to trickle into the hall. As Tony neared the entrance where the Julianno's chauffer was waiting, he stopped. As the monsignor got closer to him, cursing the whole time, the young man who once hoped to be a priest simply turned and looked directly at Coffer. He then flipped the prior off.

Coffer stopped dead in his tracks. The barrage of blasphemies and curses hurled from the monsignor's mouth filled the hallway. It was at that very instant that almost all of the parents, faculty, and student body of Augustinian Academy were converging on this spot, wanting to give their personal farewell and appreciation to the director and his staff. Coffer paused just long enough to realize what was happening. It was too late. His fury had blinded him. His eyes turned bright red. The spittle around his mouth began to slightly foam. He resembled a wild rabid animal. He lunged towards Tony, fully intending to tear him to shreds.

Tony simply stepped aside as Mr. Mays Van Williams, Dominick's newly employed chauffer, stepped between him and the deranged Coffer. If the circumstances had been different, the sight of a massive black man slamming his enormous fist into the face of the prior of Augustinian Academy would have shocked and enraged those who stood in the hallway. The crowd, however, began to clap. Even the faculty let out a cheer.

The ride to LaGuardia Airport was peaceful and uneventful. Once Tony was checked in, Mays walked with him to his departure gate. Dominick's family wanted Tony to travel home with as much dignity as he could have. They had gifted him with a first-class ticket.

"They are the most generous family I've ever met," Tony said.

"That sure is right," Mays answered. "You ain't too bad of a friend yourself. I would'a never believed that a simple trip from Columbia, South Carolina, to New York could'a brought me so much blessings."

"Mr. Van Williams," Tony said, with pure admiration, "it was because of your caring and generous spirit that you were blessed. The fact that you were willing to come to the aid of a scared and lonely stranger, even willing to open up your home to him, is the most caring thing a person could do. It's for that, and that alone, that I would do anything to help you and your family, much less the fact that you are such a good man. I can never thank you enough, Mays Van Williams."

A tear streamed across Tony's cheek. Mays Van Williams's eyes began to well up.

"I don't know what I would have done if you hadn't had Mr. Julianno call me that day. I was so desperate for a job, havin' lost mine with the city and all that. You sure were an answer to a lotta prayers."

"When I heard that they were looking for a chauffeur since Lambert had retired, you were the only name that came to mind."

"God bless you, Tony."

Mays Van Williams had no way of knowing that all that had happened to Tony Saleem in the past year, especially the last 63 days, had emptied his soul of God. Tony did not have the heart to tell him.

"Thank you, Mays," Tony simply smiled. He then turned and boarded the plane to go home.

PART THREE: THE LIFE OF THE

EX-SEMINARIAN

THIRTY-THREE

On Thursday April 9, 1975, the telephone rang in the narcotics office of the Atlanta Police Department. Sergeant Anthony Saleem was on duty.

"Sergeant Saleem, how may I help you?"

"I thought I'd let you know that he's dead." Dominick's voice was completely void of emotion.

"What? How?" Tony asked in complete disbelief.

"Well, that's what usually happens when a person loops piano wire around their neck and then ties it to a meat hook that's attached to their basement beam. They then kick the chair out from under themselves and let gravity do the rest."

"When did this happen?" Tony asked.

"You're the police sergeant!" Dominick answered. "Atlanta is still part of this country, isn't it?"

"Come on, Dom," Tony laughed. "It's ten o'clock in the morning. I've only had four cups of coffee."

"His wife found his body about three hours ago." Dominick became more serious. "The homicide guys are already on the scene. They seem to think he did it right at the crack of dawn, around 6:10 this morning."

"How do you know so much about what they're doing? You aren't at the scene are you?"

"No," Dominick laughed. "Let's just say that a certain member of the homicide squad does consultant work for me."

"Here in Atlanta, which is still part of this country, we call that *being on the take*."

"Shouldn't you advise me of my rights before you make accusations like that, Sergeant Saleem?" Dominick joked.

"I really miss you, Dom."

"Then get your ass up here and visit. I don't think you've ever met my wife, have you?"

"You know, you're right." Tony looked at the framed photo of Dominick's family, which sat on the desk next to his own family's photograph. They each had two children: a boy and a girl. "Neither one of us has ever seen each other's family except in pictures."

"And when is the last time we saw each other?" Dominick asked.

"We left that place in 1960—" Tony paused. "My God, Dom, it's been fifteen years!"

"That's my point! Don't you think we owe each other a visit before we get too old to recognize each other?"

Tony's laugh could be heard throughout the vice and narcotics office.

Herb Kashton, his supervisor, looked in to see the cause.

"You must be talking to that mafia lawyer," the lieutenant remarked. "He's the only one who can make you laugh like that."

"Tell Herb I said hello," Dominick called out, "and that he's really showing his age."

"What do you mean by that?" Herb asked, yelling at the phone in Tony's hand.

Tony smiled and handed the phone to Herb.

"They are no longer known as the mafia," Dominick said. "Their official title is La Cosa Nostra. It means Our Thing. Only the real old police, like you, still call them mafia."

"I thought you brats were supposed to respect your elders," Herb laughed. "I don't know how the NYPD feels about you, Dom, but we love you here in Atlanta."

"Thanks Lieutenant, but what brought that on? You actually sound serious."

"I am serious. We could not have caught that serial rapist and killer if it hadn't been for your help and information. I truly don't care how you got it, but it helped us remove that deranged animal from society."

"You're welcome, Lieutenant." Dominick's voice conveyed a smile.

Lieutenant Kashton handed the phone back to Tony.

"You do seem to get a lot of information," Tony commented. "The mafia—I mean, the La Cosa Nostra—must have a great intelligence division?"

"They're the same as you guys," Dominick answered. "They ask people for information. The only difference is, they don't ask as politely as you."

"Tell me more about Monsignor Coffer's suicide," Tony said, trying to get back to the original purpose of Dominick's call.

"I thought you'd never ask." Dominick Julianno, hundreds of miles away, was smiling like a Cheshire cat. "First off, he really wasn't a monsignor."

"What?"

"In fact, he wasn't even a priest. His real name was Johannes Kaffee. He was only a Brother, and a Benedictine Brother, not an Augustinian Brother. He was more than a Nazi sympathizer. He considered himself as one of their agents."

"My God, Dom, I know who he is. Bishop Peter Paul used to talk about him." Tony's voice was filled with anguish. "He was the one who turned in Dietrich Bonhoeffer. No wonder he was so scared when McCrane—Hydric—was killed."

"It was ruled a suicide," Dom said. "There was never any evidence that he was murdered."

"Dom, how did you get all of this information?" Tony knew that his question was basically rhetorical.

"That's not important," Dominick answered. "The only important thing is that it is all very factual and documented."

"I guess that's all moot now," Tony acknowledged. "He sure took the easy way out, instead of having to pay for his crimes."

"Not necessarily," Dominick paused for at least one full minute. "You know, Sister Gertrude is still alive."

"That can't be true!" Tony said, shocked. "She'd have to be almost a hundred years old."

"She's ninety six, to be exact."

"Okay, ninety six, but what does she have to do with this?"

"Everything," Dom answered. "She has a right to know what that piece of crap who impersonated a monsignor really was."

Suddenly Tony realized what Dominick was saying. The police would never say anything to her. They would leave it up to the family to tell others that it was a suicide. The newspaper or news media never printed or broadcasted a suicide unless it was a celebrity, or some other spectacular circumstances. Kaffee was not a celebrity, nor did he die under spectacular circumstances. Dominick's information would change all of that. It would strip Monsignor John Coffer, the excommunicated Augustinian priest, down to Brother Johannes Kaffee, the Nazi sympathizer and war criminal. Kaffee was not only responsible for Dietrich Bonhoeffer's execution, but also the execution of twenty two Augustinian cannons at Ettal.

"I agree, Dom," Tony said. "The information about Coffer has to be made known. It'll give us all some closure. Is there anything you need for me to do?"

"No," Dominick answered. "I'll handle everything. I'm sure you're a great cop Tony, but I'm an expert at stuff like this. It's what I do!"

Tony laughed. "Before you hang up, Dom..." Tony's voice was strained. "I think I need a favor from you."

"What do you mean by *you think*? Either you do or you don't. You know I'll do anything for you Tony. So, just ask!"

"It's going to sound crazy." Tony hesitated.

"Damn it, Tony! Are you doing this deliberately to raise my blood pressure?"

"No, Dom," Tony laughed, "although, that is a good idea. If I give you my older brother Fred's address, could you have one of your employees do something strange for me?"

"If it's real strange, I may have to do it myself, but it'll get done. What is it?"

"I want your employee, or you, to have a confrontation with him and in the middle of the confrontation, I want them to call him a nut."

"And you want me to do this because…?" Dominick was genuinely puzzled.

"It's something very personal," Tony answered. "I've been having this recurring dream about something that happened in my childhood. My brother's reaction to being called a nut will help me to resolve this thing. So, can you help me?"

"Of course," Dominick answered. "But it sounds like you're having some of this repressed memory crap that they're talking about on these television talk shows."

"My brother may go a little crazy, and I expect your employee to protect himself, but I really don't want my brother to be killed."

"Don't worry," Dominick assured Tony. "My employees are all professionals. Your brother will be okay; we'll get you his reaction. It may take me a little while to get to this, unless you're in a big hurry to find out."

"Absolutely not," Tony answered. "You're doing me a favor. Just get to it when you have time. I really do appreciate this, Dom."

Little did Anthony Saleem know that this simple, if crazy request, and what he would find out in the next few months, would change the course of his life for all eternity.

THIRTY-FOUR

It was the afternoon of February 13, 1976—Friday the 13th and the day before Valentine's Day.

"Have you gotten Barbara a Valentine's Day present, yet?" Sergeant David Grey asked Lieutenant Tony Saleem, his partner.

"Yeah, a diamond and ruby pendant," Saleem answered. Barbara was going to love this Valentine's Day.

They were both sitting in their undercover vehicle, listening to the radio transmission of the body bug their agent was wearing. Special Agent Chuck Eastman, of the Georgia Bureau of Investigation, was buying of a kilo of Mescaline from three West Georgia College students.

Agent Eastman was assigned to the Metropolitan Atlanta Narcotics Squad for this specific bust, as were fifteen other agents from various jurisdictions. Lt. Saleem was their com-division commander. Since agents from the GBI were assigned to the squad, it gave them statewide jurisdiction. This particular undercover purchase was being made in Carrollton, Georgia, forty miles west of Atlanta.

"What are you reading?" Grey asked.

"A letter from Dominick."

"Your mafia lawyer friend?'

"No," Saleem answered. "He's my La Cosa Nostra lawyer friend."

"Well, does he have any more leads for us on some rapists, killers, bank robbers, or child molesters?" Grey asked.

"No," Saleem answered. "This is more personal. It concerns my brother."

"I didn't mean to pry. Is your brother okay?"

"You're not prying. In fact you're closer to me than my brother." Saleem paused while he skimmed the document. "My brother went completely nuts when somebody called him a nut. He had to be subdued by the police. He even got violent with them. They broke his arm and his leg. He'll be going to jail on a bunch of charges after he gets out of the hospital."

"I'm sorry, man. Are you going to try to get him out of it?"

"No, I'm not," Saleem said in a determined tone. "This is something he really does deserve. My mom's gotten him out of too many consequences in the past. It's time he took responsibility for himself."

"Man, this sure is a righteous deal!" the transmitter blurted out Eastman's words.

"Well, that's the signal," Saleem said as he cranked up the car. "He's seen the dope. Alert the guys to move in and make the arrest."

"Two ninety one to all units," Sgt. Grey transmitted. "Move in. He's seen the dope!"

"Unit two ninety three clear, we're on the scene."

"Unit two ninety four clear, we have the subjects in custody."

"Unit two ninety eight, we're with ninety four, and we've seized the dope."

"It looks like they're pretty excited," Saleem said.

"I guess so," Grey answered. "They sure got there fast."

"I guess this is what it means to be a supervisor." Lt. Saleem spoke halfheartedly. ''We sit back on our experienced butts and supervise, while they do all the exciting stuff."

"I don't like this supervising crap!" Sgt. Grey was frustrated. "We should have been the first ones in there. We're always the first ones in on a bust. This is like a desk job!"

As Tony walked into the room, Sgt. Grey at his side, all three suspects were up against the wall, being searched by his investigators. Special Agent Eastman was advising the suspects of their rights. When Eastman concluded, he immediately ran towards Tony, holding out the clear plastic Ziploc bag containing the kilo of what was believed to be Mescaline, a dangerous hallucinogenic.

"Hey, Lieutenant," Eastman sounded excited. "This stuff isn't Mescaline. It field tested positive for acid."

"That's impossible!" Grey said. "They wouldn't be selling it for five thousand dollars if it was a key of acid."

"There was a DEA bulletin out at the beginning of the week," Saleem said. "The bulletin said that some drug pushers were ripped off in Los Angeles."

"I remember that!" Eastman interrupted. "They were ripped off for a large quantity of LSD. I bet these guys didn't even know what they had."

"You're probably right," Grey answered. "Did they have any weapons on them?"

"Not really," Eastman answered. "We only found one small pocket knife. There should be some weapons around here someplace. Don't worry, we'll find them, Lieutenant."

"I'm sure you will," Saleem responded. "By the way, Chuck, great job!"

"Thanks, boss."

"I hate it when he calls me that." Saleem whispered to Grey. "Let's look around the place and see if we can help them find a weapon or something."

"They can't be hidden very well," Grey responded. "This whole place is just one big room."

Saleem began to look around and clearly could see what Sgt. Grey was talking about. It was just one huge room. It was made of cinder blocks and a tin roof. The room itself was divided into three separate rooms, by means of bed sheets, hanging over two stretched clothes lines. As Saleem went past the first bed sheet divider and entered the second room, he felt a sudden chill run up his spine.

That's strange, Saleem thought. Then he noticed the shut door in the center of the wall.

Saleem drew his service revolver as he approached the door.

Why am I feeling so scared? Surely they've already checked this door by now.

As Saleem turned the knob, his heart rate spiked. He felt beads of sweat trickle down the sides of his glasses. He held the revolver directly in front of him as he jerked open the door. Tony momentarily stopped breathing. His heart skipped a beat; and he froze in place. He stared at what stood in front of him.

"Don't move!" Saleem yelled at the individual in the closet.

Tony Saleem was amazed by the fact that he could clearly see every single feature of the man—the long, stringy dirty-blond hair, the matted unkempt beard. He wore an opened red flannel shirt with a stained tee-shirt beneath. It was then that Saleem noticed the semi-automatic AR 15 rifle that he was raising. Saleem immediately cut his eyes towards the man's face and looked directly into his steel-blue eyes. This person wanted to kill him.

The man raised the rifle and aimed at Saleem's badge, which hung from his shirt pocket. It was directly over the former seminarian's heart.

Lieutenant Saleem stepped backwards and quickly glanced to his right.

Where the hell are they? He wondered where all of his officers had gone. The only one he caught a glimpse of was his partner, Sgt. Grey, secluded behind the divider sheet. He could see the tip of David Grey's gun barely poking through.

The lieutenant pulled back the hammer to his revolver and took careful aim at the man's head.

"I'm sorry," Saleem said. "I'm going to have to kill you."

At that time it was probably best that Lieutenant Tony Saleem did not know that the firing pin to his revolver was broken, causing the weapon to be inoperable. In the overall scheme of things, however, it made no difference as to the eventual outcome of the situation.

As Saleem began to put pressure on his trigger and held his sight on the man's head, he continuously looked into his eyes. There was absolutely no doubt in Saleem's mind that the deep-seated hatred and contempt in this person was about to explode on Saleem's badge and into his heart. As Saleem began to put more pressure on his trigger, he noticed a sudden change in the man's appearance. His eyes were filled with pure terror. He slowly began to lower his weapon. His fear was so great that tears were coming down his face.

"Please! Please! Don't hurt me!" the man in the closet begged. "I'm putting down my gun. I'll do anything you want. Just don't shoot!"

It was too late. Saleem had put too much pressure on the trigger. The hammer fell, but Tony's revolver misfired. Saleem breathed a sigh of relief and thanked God for the malfunction. By this time the suspect was already prostrate in front of the closet.

His arms were outstretched to the side, his palms were up, indicating that he'd been through this before.

Lt. Tony Saleem lowered his weapon as Sgt David Grey stepped out from behind the sheet with his weapon still drawn. They both walked towards the suspect.

"I'll cuff him," Grey said as he holstered his weapon.

Saleem nodded. He then noticed a strong odor of urine as he picked up the rifle next to the suspect.

"Did you piss on yourself?" Saleem asked.

"Yeah, I was scared that ya'll were going to shoot me!"

At that instant, the rest of the squad flooded into the room. Sgt. Grey was still handcuffing the suspect, but two of the agents bolted past Grey and kicked the suspect, still prostrate on the ground. Another officer smashed his foot into the suspect's head. Saleem pushed the officer away.

"That's enough of that!" Saleem's voice was filled with anger and disgust. "He's completely disarmed and handcuffed!"

Saleem and Grey lifted the suspect to his feet. Between Saleem and Grey, the man stumbled out of the one-room building to their car. After they put the suspect in the back seat, David returned to the building to make sure that all of the evidence was secured.

"What's your name?" Saleem asked.

"Gus ... Gus Messing."

"Well, Gus, I'm glad you decided to lower your rifle," Saleem said. "It could have gotten real messy in there."

The man just nodded; he appeared to be looking at something to the right of the building.

"What are you looking at?"

"Where are they?" Gus asked.

"Who are you talking about?" Saleem was puzzled.

"Your SWAT guys, I thought they wore black. Why were your guys wearing white?"

"Did you drop some of that acid?" Saleem asked.

"Hell, no, I don't do that crap." Tony Saleem looked directly into Gus Messing's eyes. He was telling the truth.

"Exactly why did you give up?" Saleem asked, their eyes still locked.

"You must have known," Gus said, very calmly, "that they were going to throw that flash grenade into the room. It scared the crap out of me; but you didn't even flinch."

Tony continued looking directly at him, but did not say a word.

"It looked and sounded like both thunder and lightning hit at the same time," Gus continued. "They must have used the distraction to come in. They just seemed to appear. There must have been twenty of 'em. That one guy, directly behind you, had to be nine feet tall. He was the biggest man I've ever seen."

Saleem could hardly believe what Gus's eyes were telling him. Gus was being truthful in every single aspect of his story.

"I've never seen a weapon like he was carrying," Gus continued. "It looked like a cross between a flame thrower and a 50 caliber machine gun. The rest of those guys were scary, but not as scary as him."

Saleem realized that Gus believed everything he was saying. The story baffled the former seminarian, but it rang true, especially to the one who was telling it.

"Did you know anything about the drugs that those three were selling?" Saleem asked.

"Hell no!" Gus Messing looked directly at Lt. Saleem. "I ain't got nothing to do with that. I was hired for two hundred bucks to protect those ass-holes. That was it!"

Saleem instantly knew that he was lying.

"So, you knew nothing about them ripping off some people out West?"

"No way, I'm involved in any rip-off, man. In fact, I've never been to Los Angeles!"

Saleem smiled. He knew that Gus was now lying through his teeth. Saleem never even mentioned Los Angeles.

"Well boss, we're ready to transport them all to jail. Are you through with this one?" Grey asked Saleem.

Saleem got out of the car and motioned for Grey to join him in front of the vehicle, out of ear-shot of Gus Messing.

"I think this guy is the mastermind of this whole thing. Ask the GBI to check him out nationwide. He's probably going to be wanted either in several states or for some serious stuff.

"What makes you think that?" Grey asked.

"It's the way he answered my questions. I feel certain he's dirty."

"I'll take care of it," Grey answered, removing Gus from the back of the vehicle.

THIRTY-FIVE

Barbara Saleem was still up waiting for her husband when Tony got home the night of February 13, 1976. She asked how his day went and if had he eaten. Tony smiled.

"Which question should I answer first?" he asked as he kissed her.

"The one that you feel is most important to you," she answered.

Her absolute wisdom amazed him. It was as if she not only could read his mind but also knew how he should answer the question, a question not yet asked even.

"I'd love some coffee," he answered, "and my day was long, but dull. We went to Carrolton. Believe me, nothing exciting ever happens in Carrolton."

Tony Saleem found out, however, that when he talked to his wife, he should always tell her the simple truth. At that very instant, the eleven o'clock news announced the drug raid in Carrolton, Georgia, and the arrest of four people. Three of those arrested were students of West Georgia College and the fourth was a fugitive from Texas wanted for three counts of homicide.

"The fugitive, according to a police spokesman," the news anchor said, "held officers at bay with a high-powered rifle. He then surrendered, without incident, to the division commander."

In that instant, Tony Saleem looked into the eyes of his precious bride and he knew the meaning of God's truth being like a double-edged sword. Barbara's eyes were beginning to well up as she began to speak.

"Why...? Why didn't you just tell me the truth?"

"I guess I was trying to protect you," was his stupid answer. He tried to take the words back the moment they were spoken, but it was too late.

"Protect me? Protect me from what? Protect me from the truth?"

"I'm sorry. I knew it was a dumb answer the moment I said it."

Barbara gently took her husband's hand and looked lovingly into his eyes. She knew he loved her and she knew, in her heart, that in his own stupid way he really thought that he was protecting her.

"Our Lord, Jesus Christ, is our protection," she softly said. "Do you believe me?"

He wasn't that stupid. He absolutely knew how to answer her.

"Yes, I do believe you." He was proud of his answer. "I'm not sure I know what you mean."

She lifted the bible, which was next to her, and placed it in his lap. She then opened it to where she had been reading. The book marker seemed to point directly to the passage. A cold sweat coved his forehead. The hair on the back of his neck began to quiver. His eyes locked in on the passage that she had been reading all day. It was underlined in red, numerous times. The water stains along the edges of the page marked her tears. The droplets at the top of the page marked the imprint of her perspiration. In that moment he knew that she truly did love him. More important, however, he knew that she was telling him the truth. Their protection was in the Lord, Jesus Christ.

Psalm ninety one, verse eleven, left its mark upon Tony's soul.

For He will give His Angels charge, concerning you,

To guard you in all your ways.

The faith that had been stripped away by the hatred and deception of John Coffer and Michael McCrane had now been restored. The love of his wife and the truth of the word of God gave Tony Saleem a new hope and a new belief.

"There really is a God!" Tony said to his wife. "He really does love us!"

Barbara smiled and kissed him gently once more. She then nodded in agreement. Nothing else was said. Nothing more needed to be said.

THIRTY-SIX

It was ten o'clock in the morning of May 2, 1993, when Tony knelt beside his mother's bed and gently held her hand. She had been in a coma for almost four days. He and Barbara were the only two there. Cecelia was in the cafeteria and Johnny was on a motorcycle road trip somewhere along the California coast. Fred was either in jail or on the run.

"I love you very much, Emma." He wasn't sure if she heard him or not.

"I know," she said in a soft and feeble voice.

"Emma! Emma! You're awake!" He started to get up. She grasped his hand even tighter. He looked at her. Her eyes were begging him to stay, to listen and do nothing else. He stopped cold and sat back down.

"I think she only wants to talk to you," Barbara said.

She raised her hand and pointed directly at Barbara, motioning her closer. She wanted her to also stay. Barbara nodded in acknowledgement. Ophelia smiled.

"Tony, I have to tell you something. I don't know how much longer I have, but I need your forgiveness. Please listen to me."

"Emma! Whatever it is, I forgive you. I love you."

"Tony. I'm begging you. Please, just listen. I have to say this!" She spoke with absolute determination.

"Emma." Barbara spoke with equal determination. "I promise you, he will shut up and listen."

"Thank you," she said, looking at Barbara and nodding. "I have always wanted you to be a priest, my son, but not for the right reasons. I knew if you were a priest that you would have to hear my confession and forgive me. You could never tell anyone what I did, and your forgiveness would be true."

Tears began to stream down her face as she grasped his hand a little tighter.

"I am so sorry, my precious son. I truly have sinned against you and God. When you were just a small child, I beat you so severely that I thought I had killed you. I beat you with a windshield wiper that your brother had handed me."

Tony blindly nodded as his wife held him close.

"Please, do not blame your brother," his mother continued. "He doesn't know what he's doing. I've always spoiled him, and I've always mistreated you. I now know that I was wrong, but it is too late. Your brother was conceived in love between your father and me. Your sister, Cecelia, was also a product of our love. The marriage between your father and me was arranged by your grandfathers. Your father's father was a mean and vicious man." Ophelia stopped and gasped for air. Tony was reaching out to her when she moved her hand indicating that she was okay.

"One night when your father was away, your grandfather came over to our house," Ophelia continued. "He said he was there to make sure I was all right." She then squeezed Tony's hand a little tighter. "I knew that he was an evil man, and I should have known that he was up to something."

Ophelia's face became pale and her eyes began to droop. Beads of sweat formed on her forehead and her hands felt moist and clammy. Tony touched her cheek, and she felt cold.

"Emma! Emma!" Tony cried out in near panic.

"I'm okay…" Her voice was barely audible. "I have to finish. Please, Barbara, pray that God lets me finish. He listens to you."

Barbara nodded and gently said, "He will also listen to you, Emma."

Ophelia only nodded. "Your grandfather came into my bedroom and he was looking at me as I was getting ready for bed. He had a satanic smile on his face. I told him to get out, or I would scream. He just smiled at me and said 'no you won't.' His eyes were dark, and he looked like he had no soul."

Ophelia began to shiver.

"Emma, stop!" Tony's voice was raspy and he was scared. "Emma, you have to stop." He was now pleading. "You can tell me some other time."

"Laht!" She said. "No! I have to tell you now!"

"Okay, Emma. Okay." Tony was now trying to calm her.

"That old bustard then told me to take off my clothes, or he would cut off the heads of my two babies. He then held up a butcher knife." Tears were now freely flowing down her cheeks. She looked directly into Tony's eyes. "That disgusting child of Satan then raped me!"

"My God …" Tony's jaw dropped open. "What are you saying?"

Tears streamed down her face. Her eyes sought comfort as they darted between Tony and Barbara.

"I told your father when he got home the next day," she continued. "He did not know what to do. He got his gun and went straight to your grandfather's house next door. He then drug him into our house. Your father must have already beaten him. He had blood running from his nose and the side of his eye. He then threw him to the ground and stuck the gun in your grandfather's mouth. He tried to pull the trigger several times, but he could not do it. Your grandfather started laughing and called him horrible names in Arabic. I begged him to kill the old man. I wanted him dead so much. Forgive me, God! I really wanted him to be dead. I then told your father that he might have impregnated me. Your father went crazy."

She stopped and was reaching for some water. Barbara got the glass from the nightstand and filled it with water. She then helped her to drink. When she had finished drinking, she took Barbara's hands and kissed them.

"I know I hated you when you first married my son, but now I truly do love you, my darling Barbara."

"I know," Barbara said, as she gently kissed her mother-in-law's hands. Ophelia smiled.

"I've never seen your father so angry before," she said, as she continued her story. "I thought he had killed your grandfather. He beat him within an inch of his life. There was blood everywhere. There was so much blood you could smell it. The whole time your grandfather said nothing. He only laughed and laughed until he could laugh no more. I thought he was dead. He was not."

"Am I his son?" Tony's question was filled with fear.

"Your father made love to me that night. He said we would never doubt that you were his son, not the son of that filthy, perverted, piece of crap. I have always wanted to believe your father, but I was never sure. That's why I mistreated you all these years. That is why I made you take off your clothes when I beat you so badly."

Her hands touched his cheek. Her breath was now coming in gasps. Her tears came gushing.

Tears also streamed down both Tony's and Barbara's faces. Their eyes looked directly into Ophelia's.

"But you know the truth, now, don't you?" Barbara was not asking a question; she was making a statement of fact.

Ophelia nodded and a slight smile played across her cracked lips.

"What is the truth, Emma?" Tony's voice was pleading.

"You are so sweet, so gentle, and so caring," she said. "There is no way that any part of your grandfather could be part of you." She barely got out the words before she started coughing.

She then began to violently gasp for air. Her coughing was so deep and convulsive it caused her fragile body to shake. She then looked at Tony as blood was dripping from her nose.

"I know that you are truly your father's son," she gasped. "He would be so proud of you."

Barbara pulled her husband even closer to her. Ophelia's breathing was becoming shallower and impossibly labored.

"I am so sorry, my son. I should have told you sooner. I've not only been a bad mother, I've also been a coward."

"Emma, don't!" Tony leaned over and gently kissed his mother on the cheek. "You've done nothing wrong. When you were hitting me, you thought you were hitting him. I forgive you, Emma. You also have to forgive him."

Her eyes widened. She was terrified. Calmness suddenly came over her as Barbara's hand gently touched her cheek. She then looked at Tony's wife and felt God's love reflected in her face. The very essence of Tony's mother changed from confusion to conviction.

"Thank you!" Her words were aimed at both of them. "I do forgive him. I know I can't force you to forgive me, my son, and that is what makes your forgiveness so much sweeter. I will always love you."

As Tony held his mother's hand, he could feel her life slip away. He also could clearly see the smile on her face as she met her Lord and Savior. He then turned to his wife and clung to her. He let himself grieve. He let himself cry as a baby who had lost his mother. He felt his wife's arms around him, and he felt very safe. She truly was a mirror of God's love.

THE END